Squatter's Rights

Squatter's Rights:

A Sam Quinton Mystery

Kevin R. Doyle

coffeetownpress

coffeetownpress

Coffeetown-Camel Press
6524 NE 181st St. #2
Kenmore, WA 98028

For more information go to: www.Coffeetownpress.com

This is a work of fiction. Names, characters, places, brands, media, and incidents are either the product of the author's imagination or are used fictitiously.

Cover design by Jeanne Gustafson

Squatter's Rights

ISBN: 978–1–603817–78–3 (Trade Paper)
ISBN: 978–1–603817–77–6 (eBook)

Printed in the United States of America

Squatter's Rights

CHAPTER ONE

On a cool Monday morning, with spring right around the corner, I was halfway through my second set of bench presses when Nicky LeBow scuttled into my gym, The Blaster. Focused on the weight, I didn't notice him at first.

Once upon a time, I could do three sets with ease, four if I pushed myself. These days, I begin to feel it somewhere around the middle of the second set and have to push to get three.

"Blondie?" came Nicky's voice on my right. I had the bar fully extended on rep six and really couldn't stand to lose my concentration.

Especially for someone like Nicky LeBow.

"Just a minute," I said before struggling through the last six reps. When the barbell finally clanged back onto the rack, I laid there for a moment staring at the ceiling, wondering where my youth had fled.

"Blondie?" Nicky said again, more plaintively this time. Sighing, I eased myself into a sitting position on the bench and grabbed a hand towel off the floor.

"What's up, Nicky?" I said as I wiped my face. "And please don't call me Blondie."

These days, only two types of people call me by that ridiculous nickname. I tolerate it from former fans and not-so-fans who know me primarily as the Blond Bomber. But the second group, friends, neighbors and acquaintances who considered it cool to be able to call me the name to my face, I didn't put up with.

Despite whatever he may have thought, LeBow definitely fell into the acquaintance category.

"I need help, Sam," Nicky said. "I'm in trouble, bad trouble."

This wasn't quite the revelation that he probably intended it to be. A three-time loser, Nicky had been in and out of trouble as long as I'd known him. And quite a bit before that.

"How bad?"

He looked around, his eyes darting back and forth to all the other people in the gym. Lisa Nolan, my manager, and our morning clients, Lisa's term, not mine, who were pressing, curling, squatting, doing yoga and roping all around the place.

For the longest time, I'd managed to keep my gym primarily a guy's place, despite the numerous good points my accountant kept bringing up about how much attracting female clientele would do for my bottom line. Lately, though, Lisa had begun to refashion the place, which had the effect of slowly attracting more women. So far, things hadn't gone too far in that direction, and men still formed the majority of our clients

Problem was, most of the guys who frequented my place weren't like the bruisers I'd hung around with back in my days in the ring. More and more I found myself getting darned near weepy with nostalgia for them.

"How bad?" I repeated, when it seemed Nicky didn't want to answer.

"Bad," he said, his voice a husky whisper. "I think this may be it for me."

I sighed. Most of Nicky's problems came in the form of overextended gambling debts, and while he occasionally found his way out to the KC metro area or St. Louis, he did the majority of his gaming within about a thirty-mile radius of Providence, Missouri, usually up at the Isle in Joneston. And whatever people may say about our gamers, they aren't nearly as connected or vicious as they could be.

I was inclined to give Nicky the cold shoulder. After all, I had both the gym and my detective agency to run, and with spring coming on our roster was filling up with people anxious to get in shape. Then he looked straight at me, his eyes nearly popping from his head in terror.

"They're gonna come for me soon, Blondie."

"Who?" I snapped.

"The cops," Nicky LeBow said in my gym on that rainy Wednesday morning. "They're going to get me for murder."

CHAPTER TWO

I had a lot of work to do that morning, most of which would hopefully help my bottom line as a gym owner. The Blaster opens at seven each morning and stays open till two am on the weekends, but during the week we shut the doors at eleven pm. I don't own a Golds-type operation, and I am not part of a franchise of gyms, filled to the brim with high-strung yuppies seeking a late-night endorphin fix.

For the first few years I had the place, it was mainly me and a hard-core male clientele: former athletes, National Guard soldiers, and quite a few cops who, for some reason or other, preferred my place to their department's own gym. I did okay, if not spectacular. At least, I was never late on the rent or utilities.

And, of course, I had a steady number of people come in just to get a look at the old Bomber. Guys mainly, though more gals than you would think, who knew me from my pro wrestling days and considered me, for some odd reason, as something of a celebrity.

So, I had a steady business, if not a great one, and while it wasn't exactly hand to mouth, some months were damned close. Then Lisa came along and started pushing me to open things up a bit. She's a good kid, with frankly a better head for business than I have, but at forty-six, I'm nowhere near the position, either financially or emotionally, to step aside and let the younger generation change things up.

Even so, I knew Nicky well enough to realize I wouldn't get any peace until I'd at least heard him out. I stopped and talked to Paul, one of my trainers, for a minute then Nicky and I headed to my office.

Nicky had been in the office once or twice, so I was at least spared the usual ooh's and ahh's that most people, especially wrestling fans, uttered when they first saw it. I never quite got it myself. It's a little cinder block room in the back of the gym, about twenty by thirty, that contains a desk (bought second hand), a three-high green file cabinet (bought third hand) and three chairs: one for me and two for any visitors.

The fairly-new chair, a tubular chrome type deal, I'd bought on a whim about six months back from a client. He owned several rental houses and had given me a bonus to express his pleasure with how quickly I identified and tracked down a former renter who'd stiffed him on about six months' rent.

The office also held a brown leather couch that had seen better days, but at least the leather wasn't peeling off.

Yet.

But I'm being a bit phony here. I know darned good and well what it is that makes newcomers to the office have hissy fits. It's the trophies and pictures. Plus, the championship Belt.

The trophies, from high school and two years of college, occupy a wooden shelf on the wall opposite the desk. Three state championships in high school, two semi-finals champs from college and one sportsmanship award from the NCAA. But while you'd think all that would be impressive, the trophies, while they get a glance, aren't what really make people swoon.

Scattered along both of the side walls are pictures, with me usually in my Blond Bomber gear, shaking hands with all sorts of actors, musicians, athletes and, in one notable one, Ted Turner himself.

But while the pictures are good, the thing that really attracts people, at least those in the know, is the Belt. It showed that at one time I was a champion. And while the MWL, the Midwest Wrestling League, wasn't exactly the big time, we mainly worked out of St. Louis and the surrounding area, to a lot of people a champion is a champion.

Even though he'd been there before, Nicky LeBow stopped for a second and stared at the wall behind my desk. He gazed at the Belt, as if it held the secret to some kind of higher power, then glanced back at me.

"Must have been a hell of a feeling," he said.

I shrugged.

"And a hell of a night. I'll be you got laid real good that night."

I shrugged again and motioned him away from my desk. I didn't feel like swapping stories with Nicky, but he was right. It had been a wild night. Unfortunately, it hadn't involved Pamela, my wife at the time, and that, as they say is a whole 'nother story.

As I sat down in my chair, Nicky slumped into one of the facing chairs, sideways and with his right leg slung over the chair arm.

That's Nicky. Why have the discipline to sit up straight when you can slump?

"Okay, dude," I said, hoping to get it over with so I could go back to running a business, "what're the cops after you for?"

"It's bad, Blondie."

"You said that before. And don't call me Blondie." For a second there, I felt like Leslie Nielsen in *Airplane*. "Just tell me what's up."

Nicky started to sit up straight, must have figured it was too much effort, and slumped again.

"It's like this Blo . . . it's like this. I've been a little short lately. That job I had lined up with Pancratio fell through, and things have been, you know, tight."

All of which meant that his make-work job with one of his cousins had been busted by the zoning contractors, and he'd managed to blow the money before he'd earned it. Most likely on the slots and the bars.

"So?" I prodded.

"So, I've been a bit short the last few weeks."

When I didn't respond, he continued.

"Actually, more than a bit. That scumbag of a landlord came by my place last week and barred my door again."

I nodded, knowing this happened about once or twice a year.

"So, I had to, you know, make other arrangements."

I tried to smother a groan, but didn't quite pull it off. "By arrangements you mean . . ."

"Squatting, yeah."

Basically, what Nicky does when funds are tight is find an occupied home with the family away for an extended time, break in, and make himself at home. He isn't malicious, doesn't cause any damage or, amazingly, take anything with him. He just makes use of the house and its amenities for a while. From what I understand, he usually even cleans the places up as much as possible, sometimes leaving them in better shape than he found them.

To the unknowing person, it may seem like quite a feat to easily find a home that would fit those criteria. But Providence ranks as one of the best small cities in the country for retirees. So we have a large number of older residents, many with highly disposable incomes, and it's not uncommon for a lot of houses in the better parts of town to be unoccupied for two or three months at a time. As to how Nicky manages to track down and pinpoint likely homes, I'd never asked and really didn't want to know, but I kind of figured he knew someone in the post office or newspaper that can give him a heads up when someone wants their mail or home delivery stopped.

Nicky calls it squatting, but anyone else would call it breaking and entering. "And?" I prodded him again.

"So, I came upon this really sweet deal. It's a two-story place, two older people with them long gone. I think the guy's a doctor or something, guy named Richards, and he and the missus took off for a month or so. Way I get it from a few little clues I found, they went to France."

"Nobody house sitting for them?" I asked.

Nicky shrugged.

"Seems not. Judging by the looks of the place, it was a spur of the moment thing. These two must be loaded. So, like I say, I've been there for about a week now, and last Friday Joey

Garzone, you know Joey?" When I didn't bother to answer, he continued, "Anyway, Joey and I headed out to the Isle and, well, we did pretty good."

I glanced at the clock. It was coming on to eleven, and I had a lot to do.

"Nicky," I said, "fascinating as all this is, could you please get to the goddamned point? I've got a business to run here."

"Sure, Sam, sure. So anyway, Joey and I did pretty good Friday and we had enough to really tie one on. We ended up staying up there with his cousin, who has a house out that way. Found us a couple of blondes. Hell, we had a time."

The Isle is our area's premier casino, located in a smallish town about thirty miles away. Nicky had a lot of "hell of times" out there, but he usually ended up even more broke than when he started.

If I hadn't still been wearing the sweat shirt from my work-out I would have peeled back my sleeve to look at my watch. But my watch was still in my gym bag, where I'd dropped it on the floor when we came in.

"The point, Nicky."

"Right, right. The point is, we had such a good time that I ended up not going home until this morning."

I decided not to point out that "home" was a fairy relative term the way he meant it. "Then what's the problem?" I asked.

Nicky came out of his slouch and placed his hands on his thighs.

"When I got there, the place was surrounded by cops. There were at least four cop cars outside those people's house, and a whole bunch of them going in and out."

I stayed quiet. All the slackness had gone out of his face. Rather than look at me, his eyes had gone behind me and fixed themselves on the Belt. Like a lot of people, he probably thought the Belt meant that I'd once been the top of my field, when in reality it only meant that once upon a time the bookers had decided I should have my moment in the spotlight.

My very brief moment.

"I didn't want to hang around there. I mean, I obviously don't quite fit into the neighborhood, you know. But I figured I had to know what was going on in that house. I mean, when I left it Friday afternoon everything was fine."

"So?" By now, I felt as if I'd spent my entire morning prodding Nicky to get to it.

"I talked to a few of the neighbors hanging around, slick as could be, and it turns out that they'd found a body in there. A dead body."

I passed on pointing out that finding a live body wouldn't be all that interesting. "Well," Nicky continued, "as soon as I heard that I lit out of there as quietly as I could. Made my way to Kimmie's diner a couple of miles away and sat down to think things through. Then, just as I'm trying to sort it out, a local newsbreak comes on their TV they've got up in the corner. You know how a lot of old duffers like to hang around Kimmie's in the morning, right? This place has a TV they keep tuned to *Good Morning America* and . . ."

"Nicky!" My limit had finally been reached. "Get to it, dammit." He jumped, but Nicky tends to jump at the sight of a cockroach.

"Okay, Sam, okay." The fact that he was using my actual name gave an indication of how upset he was becoming. "So, they've got the sound off on the TV, but they got the caption thing going. You know, the one for old people who can't hear anymore." I let that one slide as well. "And it turns out that someone called the cops this morning saying they heard screams coming from the house. When the cops get there, they break in and find this girl, they said looked like mid-twenties, murdered in the living room."

He finally wound down and stood there looking at me.

"Had they ID'd the girl?" I asked.

"Didn't say nothing on the morning news, but I don't know about by now."

I drummed my fingers on my desk.

Nicky looked past me at the Belt. A cheap strip of tin and gold leaf, scrolled with some fancy fonts, stitched on a broad swath of artificial leather, colored red with gold edges. It probably cost all of twenty dollars to make, back in the nineties, and in the harsh office lighting you could see some of the gold leaf beginning to tarnish.

Just a cheap trinket. Hell, at the house shows the MWL used to sell indistinguishable items for fifteen dollars. Yet the Belt always held that fascination, and I figured that Nicky was staring at it like that to get his mind off his very real troubles.

Yeah, it was obvious that, regardless of how I'd felt earlier, Nicky LeBow was in big, big trouble.

"How long did you say you were you squatting in that house?"

He tore his eyes from the Belt and looked my way. His eyes glistened. "Almost a week," he said.

"Then, the place is lousy with your DNA and prints," I said. He nodded, the glisten more pronounced now.

"I didn't come here 'cause you own a gym," he said.

I frowned. It had been nearly a month since I'd had a case, and in that time the gym had been doing pretty well. We'd run a couple of specials in the last few weeks and drawn in nearly fifty new year-long members. It was enough of a perk up that I'd started considering, as I do two or three times a year, about hanging up my P.I. license and just concentrating on the gym. When I'd first got my license a few years back, figuring I'd found my new career, I hadn't intended to inherit a gym at the same time. I found myself wavering back and forth on which business to concentrate on, usually determined by which is more profitable at any given time.

Nicky was a bit of a mess. But he wasn't a bad guy, and he did seem to be in a jam. "Of course, you're on file with the cops," I said.

The poor sap shrugged again and looked down at the floor.

"Okay," I said. "Why don't you hang out here for a while. Duck in the back if anyone official looking comes along, and I'll see what I can do."

"How much . . . how much do you charge, Sam?"

Like I said, the gym had had a good month.

"Let's see what I can do, if anything, and we'll go from there." Nicky gave a little smile, probably more to reassure himself than me.

"I never in my life thought I'd have the Blond Bomber fighting for me," he said.

Now it was me glancing at the Belt.

"Nicky," I said, "the Bomber was just a character. A role I played. That's not who I am, or was."

He nodded, but I could tell he didn't agree.

That's how it goes. To so many of them I'll always be the Blond Bomber, former pro wrestling champ, never just plain old Sam Quinton.

CHAPTER THREE

A few years back, what remained of Midwest Wrestling League had been bought out by one of the bigger federations, the same one for which I'd briefly worked before blowing out my left knee for the third time. (Third and final time as it turned out. The doctors gave me an ultimatum at that point. Either hang it up or be walking with a cane the rest of my life.) At the time of the buyout, well past its prime years, MWL was lucky to put on a show a month, usually in some small-town high school gym.

The new owners, to get some mileage out of what was essentially a fire sale, had gone on a blitz, promoting the hell out of the buyout. One of those "return to the glory days" type deals.

About six months after the buyout, I received a check in the mail for a pretty decent sum, royalties for some merchandise bearing my likeness and some DVD's of my old matches. There were enough figures to the left of the decimal point that I paid off the rest of my loan for the gym, socked some away in a small mutual fund, and bought myself a brand-new Jeep Cherokee. Cashmere pearl color and all the bells and whistles.

Looking back, probably not the best of purchases. Everyone I knew started thinking I'd come into serious money. For a while there, I kept hearing a rumor that I'd signed a contract with MWL's new owners to start appearing on some of their cable shows.

Hardly.

Still, I felt a lot better pulling up to a crime scene in the Cherokee than in the Bundymobile Dodge I'd had before. I had to park about two blocks away from the house, and what with all of the cops, reporters, crime scene people and just regular gawkers, it took ten minutes to get up to the yellow police tape that cordoned off the front yard.

"Sir?"

The cop who accosted me was young, enough so that I squinted to see if he still had pimples.

Unfolding my wallet, I held out my license for the kid.

Now it was his turn to squint. Providence isn't that big of a city, a hundred thousand give or take. There aren't a whole lot of PI's in town, and few of us ever mix in active police work.

Most of the guys and gals spend their time doing the usual work of skip tracing, chasing down runaways and gathering info for divorce proceedings.

No reason at all for the kid to know me. Then again . . .

"Hey," the young cop said, "aren't you . . ."

"Yep," I said.

Sam Quinton, aka The Blond Bomber. Gym owner, private investigator and former pro wrestling champion.

Ain't diversity a heck of a thing.

"Lt. Kronberg around?" I asked.

"Naw. He's out of town at some conference or something."

"What about Sgt. Nichols?"

Providence only had a few more police detectives than it did PI's. If I stood there naming off names for a few more seconds I'd hit on whoever was running the case.

"Yeah," the kid replied, "Nichols is inside the house there. But you know I can't let you in."

"I understand," I said. "But if you could just give him my name and let him know I'm out here, I'd appreciate it."

The kid cop looked at me again.

"I don't quite get this. You were a champ, right? In the big time?"

"A champ, yes. The big time, not so much." I answered.

"And now you're a detective?"

"Among other things." I grinned at the kid. "Hard to believe, huh?"

He looked me over again. I stand six three, a little over two hundred and twenty-five pounds. At forty-six I've managed to retain the long, flowing blond hair that gave me my ring name, but whenever I look in the mirror I can't avoid the streaks of gray running through. No doubt my attire, faded Levi's, a gym shirt with the sleeves cut off and Skechers, didn't exactly reassure him as to my seriousness.

"Look, kid," I tried again, "it's like a fifty-foot walk. Sure, Nichols is probably busy, but just say my name, and if he says go, I go. What's the big deal?"

The young cop thought it over, then motioned to another patrolman standing about twenty feet away.

"Cover me for a sec here, okay?"

I smiled my thanks to my new friend.

* * *

Born and bred in Centreville, a dot on the map a few miles outside of Providence, Josh Nichols had started his career with the St. Louis cops. He shouldn't have been successful on the streets. Physically, he's average in almost every way, but his blond hair, green eyes and baby face always disarms people, not letting them imagine just how tough he can be. Josh worked as a patrolman in St. Louis for five years, and like most young cops did some security work on the side to make ends meet.

This was around the time I was winding down in the MWL, and while we did shows all around the middle of the country, St. Louis was our company headquarters and where most of our, admittedly few, TV shows were taped.

Patrolman Nichols ended up with a fairly steady gig doing security for us, so he and I kept bumping into each other. We'd occasionally meet up in a bar after a show, and even double dated once or twice, at least when I could do so without my ex-wife finding out. Then, as he started his sixth year with the SLPD, his mom came down sick and he moved back to Providence to be as close as possible.

We weren't exactly best buds or anything, but when I retired from wrestling we pretty soon began crossing paths again. Without any real skills, I'd started taking bouncing jobs at clubs to pay the bills. The bouncing led to a job offer from Duke Prowder, a local P.I., and things kind of went from there.

In a twist I hadn't seen coming, about the time I got my license and was ready to open my own shop, I inherited the gym from an old friend who'd passed away. In no time at all I'd gone from no real prospects to two businesses, one a bit more viable than the other. Nichols, in plainclothes for a couple of years at the time, even wrote one of the mandatory three reference letters that helped me snag my PI license.

My new best bud had only been in the house about thirty seconds when he reemerged, Detective Sergeant Nichols in tow. Nichols took one look, as if to assure himself it was in fact me, then rolled his eyes.

Now came the tricky part.

"What are you doing here?" Nichols asked as he came my way.

"Just happened to be passing by," I said, "and saw all the commotion. Got kind of curious about it."

"Kind of curious, huh? Try again, buddy. You usually come up with a better line than that."

"Okay," I said, shrugging as modestly as I could, "I had an appointment with Dr. Richards, and got here to see all of this." I waved my arms to encompass the general area.

"Why?"

"I'm not sure. He called and said he may have a job for me and could I spare about half an hour. I said yes, and here I am."

Nichols looked at me. A five-year old would pick up right away on the obvious flaw in my story, but I wanted to get him interested enough to talk to me.

"Come inside the rope, Sam, and let's have a chat."

I ducked under the yellow barrier tape and followed Nichols up the driveway to the house, wondering just how long he would wait to call my bluff.

We headed into the house and entered a maelstrom of activity. Everywhere I looked I saw uniformed cops, plainclothes and lab techs. Two different photographers were moving in and out of the various rooms snapping pictures; a handful of young people in white coats were gathering samples of carpets, food particles and hairs; and two folks from the medical examiner's office huddled around a young female body splayed out on the large sofa made of dark, mahogany-colored leather.

"Richards called you this morning, right?" Nichols asked without turning to look at me.

"Well . . ." I began

"See, there's a problem here, Sam. Namely the mister and missus of this place are out of the country and have been for a couple of weeks. So I really don't see how they'd expect to meet up with you this morning."

I could have stalled by pretending to be confused. After all, I have had clients lie upon occasion, and every now and then misrepresent their identity. But while I knew that sooner or later, I'd have to turn Nicky over to them, I wanted as much info as I could get before I did so.

"So here's what I'm thinking," Nichols continued when I didn't answer him, "I'm thinking that you tell me right now what you're doing here before I run you in for interfering with an investigation."

I wasn't exactly sure how I'd been interfering, but I didn't see the value in pressing that point with him.

"Who's the girl?" I asked.

Nichols sighed and rubbed his face.

"Anybody ever point out that you're just as tenacious in private life as you were in the ring?"

I noticed a couple of the crime scene people pointing my way and whispering.

Probably wouldn't be as impressed with my presence if I

mentioned that lately I was struggling to get through my bench presses.

"Who is she?" I repeated.

"We don't know yet," Nichols said. "There wasn't any purse around, no other kind of ID, at least not for her. When we got hold of Richards, we sent a picture to his phone, but neither he or his wife knew her."

"Or so they said," I pointed out. Nichols nodded.

"But we think we know what she was doing here."

"Oh?" I kept my voice as neutral as possible.

"Yeah. Kind of looks like somebody's been living here. At least one man, judging by the stuff we found, and we figure she may have been staying here as well. Or maybe he picked her up and brought her back here for some fun."

"And things got out of hand?" I asked. "It's a theory."

I could tell by his expression that my friend had put two and two together and come up with the obvious sum.

"Your turn now, and no more stalling. What are you really doing here? And don't give me any crap about Ben Richards calling you. He's a seventy-four-year-old retired podiatrist. So unless he woke up in Paris this morning and decided that he wanted to become a member at your gym . . ."

"Two more questions," I said, "and then I'm all yours."

"No more questions, Sam. And don't try to smooze me with any of your nostalgic crap. This is an active murder scene and I want to know why you're here."

"How was she killed?" I put my best "Blond Bomber" grin on my face, hoping to con him despite his protestations.

The grin worked better back in the days when my hair was actually blond instead of the grayish mix it is now.

"Strangled, manually. At least as far as we can tell by eyeballing. Once Charlie there gets her on the table, it may look different, but the visual marks seem to bear it out. Now for the last time . . ."

"Okay, okay. Just do me a favor and hear me all the way out before you start yelling."

"Forget yelling. I'll just slap the cuffs on you and have your errand boy out there haul your ass downtown if you don't spill."

I'd felt a little tense there for a while, but with Nichols telling me that the girl was strangled, I was feeling better. No matter how much I tried, I couldn't fix in my mind the image of Nicky LeBow having any gumption, or strength for that matter, to strangle anyone, especially not manually.

Still, considering his shady past, I felt obligated to provide as much space as possible. But there was one thing I needed to know before I jumped in with both feet.

"Time of death?" I ventured.

"Dammit, Sam. Would you just . . ."

"Give me time of death, Josh. Honest. Then I'll spill."

Nichols ran his fingers through his hair, and for a moment I thought I'd pushed it too far.

"You know we can't tell for sure until they get her on the table," he said. "And even then not so much. But we've gotten a ballpark guess, going mainly by the stench that hit the first guys on scene, is sometime late Friday, early Saturday."

In other words, when Nicky would have an alibi, though a far from ironclad one.

"Okay," I said, "my turn. But why don't we go outside for some privacy?"

As we headed out, I figured that I was about to either save or sink my client, and possibly myself as well. Nicky wasn't the most standup citizen, and as soon as Nichols heard his name in association with this, he'd be unhooking the cuffs from his belt.

During my pro wrestling days, I'd been a master of the "sell," otherwise known as getting people to go along with the reality you were trying to depict. I was going to need all my selling skills now, if I was going to get Nicky out of this.

But I'd been retired a heck of a long time.

CHAPTER FOUR

"Nicky freakin' LeBow?" Nichols said.

We hadn't stayed at the house long. As soon as we'd gotten on the porch the handful of press people had recognized Nichols and headed our way.

So rather than try to find a section of the Richards yard where we could talk in private, we'd climbed into my Cherokee and driven about a dozen blocks to a biker's bar. It was late enough for it to have just opened, but early enough that we were the only patrons.

Even so, Nichols and I took a booth in the far back, with the cop insisting that he had ten minutes tops before he had to get back to the crime scene. When I laid out the basics for him, he loosened up and leaned back in the booth, leading me to think that I'd just gotten an extension on that ten-minute time frame.

"Yeah," I said, "Nicky LeBow."

"So, he's back to his house crashing, huh?"

I shrugged, having no way to logically defend the guy.

"And he came to you rather than come in to us, right?" Nicholas asked.

"Come on, Josh. If you had his record, would you casually walk into the station? He didn't make a run for it, just looked somewhere for a little comfort."

"He has to come in," Nichols said.

"Of course. And I'll bring him in. I just want to ensure that he'll be treated right. I know, you know and every damned cop on the street knows that what happened to that girl isn't Nicky's style."

Nichols drummed his fingers on the table for a minute. Even though we were the only two people in the place, no one came over to serve us. When we'd entered Nichols had thrown the bartender a look that signaled to leave us alone.

Sighing, he steepled his fingers in front of him.

"No," he said, "I don't see this as his sort of thing. We're going to have to run some checks, and he's going to be in trouble for crashing in the house, but just tell him we want him to come in as a witness."

"And you'll treat him okay?"

"I may hassle him a bit to get my point across, but as long as he's on the level with me he'll be okay. Though I can't vouch for what the homeowners may want to do to him."

"Which leaves you with a hell of a problem," I said.

"No shit, Sam. But I was the one who caught it, so it's my problem."

"Are the owners coming back?" I asked.

Nichols started to answer, then caught himself.

"That's police business, bud, and no concern of yours. Bring your client in so we can get him straightened out and go on your way. As far as that goes, he may have some nugget of information that will help us out, for which I'd be eternally grateful."

We got up and left the bar, the bartender studiously ignoring us as we walked out. "Don't bother taking me back," Nichols said. "I'll call for a squad car. Just get back to your gym and get your guy downtown. I'll be along quick as I can, but don't be surprised if you have to wait for a while."

I opened the door and climbed into the Cherokee.

"By the way," Nichols called out as I looked back, "how much is old Nick paying you for this little favor?"

I shook my head, rolled my eyes, fired up the ignition and headed off to collect my client.

CHAPTER FIVE

"I sure appreciate this, Blondie."

It was shortly after four o'clock, and we'd just come off the elevator into the parking garage. The Providence PD building only has two stories with the garage across the street. As Nicky and I came off the elevators I could look out the entranceway and see the beginning of late afternoon traffic filling up the street.

A cool little BBQ shack sat a block away, and I was considering ducking in there for an early dinner before heading back to the gym. Because of dealing with Nicky, my workday was pretty much shot anyway.

"I mean it," he repeated. "I sure do appreciate this."

"Don't worry about it," I said. "Just be available to Nichols. He's cutting you a hell of a break, so make sure he knows how to get ahold of you."

"Oh, I will, don't worry about that."

Nichols had shown up at the station about twenty minutes after Nicky and me. He started off acting like he was going to pull out a rubber hose, but I figured he was only trying to intimidate Nicky into being totally truthful, so I let it go. Not that I could have done much as it was. I wasn't there as Nicky's legal representative. Nichols was letting me hang around as a courtesy.

Once they had Nicky properly cowed, and after he assured

them that he didn't want an attorney around, the real work began.

It was a long interview, with Nicky being, as far as I could tell, up front and honest. He knew he was incriminating himself in terms of breaking and entering the Richards's home, plus whatever charges would go along with that. Nichols had assured me, and I'd assured Nicky, that as long as he gave them whatever he could about the murder he'd be clear on that.

Nichols hadn't mentioned that Nicky was putting himself on the record with all kinds of stuff that could lead to a civil suit if Dr. Richards and his wife chose to pursue such a course.

He gave the cops the same story, in the main, that he'd given me. He went into a lot more detail with them, only hedging when it came to providing the names of the people he'd spent the weekend with. But between Nichols frowning at him, and another detective pointing out that they'd spent the weekend at the Isle, a completely legit casino, Nicky gave in and provided the names.

They took his fingerprints in order to narrow down any stranger prints in the house, but I figured that since they had his prints on file anyway that was just another bit of turning the screws just because they could. They also took a mouth swab for DNA.

By the time all that was finished, Nicky looked like something dragged in by whatever the cat had dragged in. At least he was free, if not exactly clear. And he still had the prospect looming over him of the Richards's coming back to the States sometime in the next day or so.

"Where are you going to go, Nicky? You sure can't go back to living at that house."

"Aw, don't worry, Blondie. I can make some arrangements okay."

"Don't go squatting again. Josh and his people took it easy on you today, but if you go back to . . ."

"Don't worry about that. I've got a couple of guys who'll let me crash until I get some funds."

It occurred to me that if he knew some people he could stay with, he should have done so rather than break into some strangers' house. But I didn't feel much like arguing the point. I'd been with Nicky for nearly the entire day, and my taste buds were clamoring for BBQ.

"Can I give you a lift, somewhere?" I asked, silently wishing he'd say no.

"Naw, that's okay. I kind of feel like stretching my legs after being shut up in there all day. I'll see you later."

"Okay," I said, as I turned to head to my car.

"Oh, Blondie."

Grimacing, fearing he'd changed his mind about the ride, I turned back. "Yeah?"

"I guess I owe you something for today, huh?"

"Don't worry about it," I said. "Catch me down the line."

"I will. I've got something lined up for next week, and if it turns out like I think, I'll be able to do right by you."

"Good enough," I said as I climbed in the Cherokee, the thought of BBQ now overwhelming any other consideration

He waved at me as I drove out of the garage.

I was sure that, in his own way, Nicky meant well, but I wasn't holding my breath for him to "do right" by me.

CHAPTER SIX

I got into the gym a little after seven the next morning. Lisa Nolan was already hard at it, cleaning some of the equipment that she hadn't gotten to the day before. Lisa is about twenty-five, five' one, with red hair and green eyes. She also has what some of my old-time ring pals would have called a bodacious figure. She knows that and, without being slutty about it, dresses to impress, at least around the gym. She's quite a lure for the male members, but despite first impressions she's all business.

Lisa used to be a member. About two years ago she showed up one day doing her best to cover up some bruising around the eyes. It took some doing, but I managed to get out of her that her boyfriend, and business partner in a small vegetarian café, had been in the habit, at least once a month, of knocking her around.

It didn't take much convincing for me to visit said boyfriend at their apartment. I had to briefly slip into Blond Bomber mode, but before long he saw the error of his ways and promised to leave her alone. In short order, Lisa split with the heel and sold out her part of the business, but that left her with a couple of major problems, namely unemployment and homelessness.

I managed to fix both of those in the short term. Gave her a job working at the gym, doing the cleaning and the books for the most part. It didn't pay much, but I also had an unused room upstairs that we converted into a studio apartment.

That "short-term fix," though, turned out to last a lot longer than I thought. Lisa got along with the members so well, and was so meticulous in her job, that within six months I said the hell with it and made her manager. The bump in pay allowed her to get her own apartment in one of the student housing complexes close to the university.

For quite a while now she'd had her eye on getting a place downtown. Lately, quite a few developers have thrown up luxury places downtown, hoping to cash in on the recent boom in student population at the university.

Except that after only a few years that boom is already turning into a bust, and with fewer and fewer students coming each year, some of those developers, after tying up traffic, inconveniencing pedestrians and throwing the entire central area into turmoil, may end up with a whole lot of fancy ass places they can't rent. After all, would any sensible Midwesterner pay over a thousand dollars a month for an *apartment*?

Lisa's got a plan to wait another half year or so, till the bust becomes official, then see if she can cash in on reduced rent. I've offered to let her keep on staying in the upstairs studio, but she said that she needed to start making her own life again and didn't want it to completely revolve around work.

A young woman with quite a head on her shoulders.

An even dozen members were already working out when I got there, all older, gray-haired fellows. We open at six, though we don't usually get busy till midday, so there's always a few of the oldsters who get there early to avoid the crowd, and a lot of those guys are in better shape than some men a third their age.

I stood off to the side for a while and watched Dwight, a shy man in his mid-sixties, doing bench presses. I couldn't help but notice that he was pressing the same poundage I'd been working on yesterday and seeming to have a lot less trouble with it.

About the time he began his fourth set, I shook my head in disgust and walked over to Lisa.

"Sorry about ditching out of here yesterday," I said. "Didn't mean to be gone the whole time."

She nodded, her ponytail flipping a bit as she did so.

"No problem. It was fairly quiet. Even managed to get last month's accounts caught up. By the way, haven't you been checking your messages? Nichols has called three times already this morning."

I reached into my jeans pocket and pulled out my phone.

"Dammit," I said, "charge is down."

"Tell me again, boss. How did you manage to keep two businesses afloat before I came along?"

"Don't get cocky," I told her. "You're only responsible for keeping one of the companies going. Did he say what he wanted?"

"Naw, but he sounded awful pissed. A little bit more each time he called. I'd get hold of him if I were you."

I nodded and headed towards my office. As soon as I got inside I picked up the desk phone and called Nichols's cell number.

"Where the hell you been?" was his opening line, and he sounded more put out than I could remember him ever being.

"Dead phone," I replied. "Sorry."

"Forget sorry, bud, and get your ass out here right now."

"Get where? You at the station?"

"No, big guy. I'm not at the station. We're at the rear side of Rhiner Hall."

"Why do I need to go there, Josh?"

"Just get down here, Blondie. And make it fast. We've got one hell of a problem here."

"Josh," I said, by now not trying to keep the exasperation out of my tone, "I just got to work. What's the problem?"

"It's your buddy from yesterday. And he's not looking too good right now."

CHAPTER SEVEN

Providence is a college town, over the last ten years or so the population creeping over a hundred thousand people. We've got three main campuses within the city limits, all within a few miles of downtown, and a whole host of satellite sites for tech schools, private schools and community colleges. Yet with all that, one main university gives the city its identity, so much so that almost everyone who lives here knows the name of all the buildings, halls and stadiums by heart.

Nichols only had to mention Rhiner Hall and within eight minutes from leaving my gym I was pulling up, for the second time in two days, to a crime scene.

Rhiner has been around for nearly two centuries, since the founding of the school itself, and has gone through all sorts of evolutions and changes over the years. For the last four or five decades, it's served as the university's primary performing arts center.

I parked close to a tiny patch of parking lot behind the hall, one used by employees. Where the lot backed up against the hall's rear wall sat two Dumpsters, the center of all the official activity.

I got out of the Cherokee and headed over. A young uniform started to hold me up, but Nichols spotted me and waved him away.

We met each other at the halfway point to the Dumpsters.

"Bad news here, Sam."

I'd had the drive over to get myself psyched up, and noticing all the official vehicles, including once again a tech van and ambulance idling nearby, I pretty much figured what he had to show me.

"Can I see him?" I asked.

Nichols shrugged and we headed over.

I'm not a firearms expert. Some hunting with my uncle when I was a kid, and of course I'd had some training back when I'd started working with Duke Prowder, the man who mentored me in the detective biz. So when it comes to guns I'm not a novice, but I'm no pro.

Whoever had done in Nicky LeBow had been a pro.

He was wearing the same clothes he'd had on when we parted ways the evening before. Positioned back up against the wall, scrunched in between the two trash containers, he looked as if he'd simply decided to sit down and rest his back against the wall.

With his arms and legs splayed to the side, I'd almost have imagined he was sleeping off a binge, except for the three blood-soaked holes in his chest.

"Three shots,"I said.

"Far as we can tell without moving him around, and we're not ready to do that yet. But yeah, at least three."

I turned and gazed around the area, taking in as much of the environment as I could, including the clustered knot of rubberneckers off by the corner of the Hall.

None of it felt right.

"Doesn't make sense, Josh," I said. "What would Nicky have been doing in this area? He'd have absolutely no reason to be anywhere around the campus."

"How'd you leave him yesterday?" Nichols asked.

"He was shaken up, you guys did a good job with that, but he seemed relieved and a lot more relaxed than when he first walked into the gym. Seemed to think that most of his problems were behind him."

"Where was he going?"

"Said that he knew a couple of guys who could put him up for a few nights, and that he'd be in touch with me later. I warned him not to go back to house crashing, at least for a while, and that was it."

Nichols shook his head and looked back at the corpse slouched against the brick wall.

"For a guy who never had a bit of violence on his sheet, LeBow sure seems to have been mixed up in something bad."

"Maybe," I said, "or maybe more than one thing."

Nichols turned back to me.

"Meaning what?"

"Just that maybe the two of them, the dead girl and Nicky getting his, aren't connected. Maybe it's just a case of really bad coincidence."

The statement felt hollow even as I spoke it. Judging by Nichols's frown, he didn't buy it any more than I did.

"You ID the girl yet?" I asked.

Nichols nodded, and his face looked even more sour.

"Name's Tammy Dodger, aka Tam O' Shanter. Travels the state working in the clubs, mainly down at Dorsey's."

Now I made a face. Dorsey's was probably our best known, and most notorious "gentleman's club." Something niggled at my brain, but I couldn't quite pin it down.

"If she worked in the business," I asked, "what the heck would she be doing with a guy like Nicky? It was usually about once a decade that he had more than two bills to rub together at any given time."

Nichols shrugged, but he was only half paying attention to me. A white station wagon had pulled up with the county emblem on the doors. A good-looking redhead, who stood about five' eight or so, got out.

Nichols walked over and chatted with the ME for a bit, leaving me standing alone and trying to look like I belonged there. Having nothing better to do, I scanned the crowd. At one point, my gaze stopped on a dark, hulking fellow who looked like a linebacker about ten years past his prime. Wearing jeans, tee-shirt and black biker's jacket, he wasn't exactly the sort you'd expect to see wandering the grounds of academe, at least not in the daytime.

I continued looking over the crowd, the same bunch that gathers every time something promises to be exciting but isn't, and didn't see anyone else out of the ordinary. When I looked for the Hulk in Leather again, he'd disappeared on me.

That little niggle that I'd gotten when Nichols mentioned Dorsey's had now blossomed into a full-throated warning siren as Nichols came back over my way.

"You might as well take off, Sam. I'll . . ."

"Paddy O'Brien," I said.

Nichols now wore the expression of a first-timer who'd gotten to the bottom of the Tequila bottle and found that the worm was still alive.

"Yeah," he said, "I was wondering how long before you made that connection."

"Does Paddy still own Dorsey's?" I asked.

"You mean does his name appear on the lease and monthly bills? Hell, no. Is he ever spotted around the place during normal business hours? Of course not. But is he the guy that all the money flows to? Far as we know he still is."

"Who's the manager out there now?"

Nichols peered at me, and I got the unsettling feel that he was considering slapping the cuffs on me and hauling me off "for my own protection."

"Just what business is that of yours?"

Shrugging, I gave him the "aw shucks" look. "Aw shucks" had been one of my best faces, back in my wrestling days. I'd use it to connote harmlessness, resignation and just wanting to be friends right before I banged a guy over the head with a steel chair.

"Just curious," I said.

"Yeah right. Listen up, Sam. Our little Mayberry here has had two murders in the last three days. And while neither of them were exactly top-flight citizens, they're also not the usual gangbangers plinking away at each other. There's going to be crap coming down like you can't believe. So, do me a favor. Your client there," he gestured over towards where the red- headed ME was still moving around and working with the body, "is dead. And whether there's one killer here or two, you don't want to be around it. Go home. Or go back to the gym and do some honest work. Maybe do a skip trace or two, but whatever the hell's going on here, you don't want to be involved in this."

I nodded my head, and in doing so happened to glance at the street that ran along the left side of Rhiner. A rusted Ford Bronco was moving down the street, and it was hard to tell from that distance, but the driver looked like the biker I'd seen in the crowd.

Nichols was right. My only involvement in any of this was through Nicky, and he was lying dead a few feet away.

"You're right," I said. "After all, when you think about it this has nothing to do with me."

As I walked away and back to my car, I could feel Nichols's eyes on me. I didn't know how well, if at all, I'd fooled him. But one thought was uppermost in my mind.

It had been a long, long time since I'd sat down with Paddy O'Brien.

CHAPTER EIGHT

I stopped by the gym to check in with Lisa. Things had picked up in the short time I'd been gone. Already, just shy of nine o'clock, at least half of the machines in use and the yoga class almost full. I still had trouble reconciling yoga with my view of what a gym should be, but the one time I brought it up, Lisa gave me a scornful look.

"If the dinosaurs had learned to duck," she'd said, "they'd maybe still be around."

Smart kid. If she got any smarter I'd have to make her a partner.

Plus, having the gym's bank balance in the black each month made me feel more than amenable to changing with the times.

Assured that she had everything under control, I headed to my office. I'm old fashioned enough to have an actual telephone in my office with an honest-to-God answering machine hooked up to it.

Maybe I should think more about Lisa's point about the dinosaurs.

The machine showed that I had four messages since the last time I'd checked. I hit the switch and listened to them while I changed clothes.

I'd shown up that morning wearing regular gym clothing, which would have been fine for a normal work day. But I'd come to a decision talking to Nichols out behind Rhiner Hall, and one didn't call on the local Godfather wearing sweats.

One message was from my accountant, asking me to call whenever I got the chance. His tone was laconic enough that I figured it wasn't anything major, probably just wanting to give me an end-of-the-month rundown on my current finances. I knew the gym was doing okay while the PI business was, to put it charitably, sporadic. But with the overhead on the latter almost non-existent, I figured I could wait to talk to him.

Another call was from a woman I'd met at a bar a couple of weeks back, wanting to know if I wanted to get together this weekend. I made a note on my desk calendar to call her if I was free, meaning if I got this LeBow mess cleared up in time. Considering that I was about to go visit Paddy O'Brien, I wanted to know exactly where I stood before any civilians were seen with me in public.

The last two calls were hangups, about normal for a given day. Providence only has a couple of prefix exchanges, we're basically a three-ZIP code-town, and it's not uncommon for someone to call the wrong number.

I changed from my sweats into jeans, a tee-shirt and a leather jacket, almost the same getup as the man I'd spotted hulking around Rhiner Hall. I'm getting a bit long in the tooth to wear clothing like that, but most people I've known for any length of time expect me to still look and act like the Blond Bomber they remember from the days of yore.

The clothing I can deal with, but no way do I go around in public acting like the buffoon I'd played in the ring for so many years. As the greatest movie star of all time said in one of his best films, a man's got to know his limitations.

I made my way out of the gym and into the Cherokee. I knew where I was going, even though I hadn't been there in a couple of years. Just a short jog from downtown, where the gym's located, to the Interstate, and in no time at all I was flying down the I, headed west and about twenty miles outside of town.

I had no way of knowing if I'd find Paddy at his place, seeing as how it was one of probably half a dozen homes that I figured he owned. Paddy's exact property and worth had always been a source of conjecture among the local, state and federal law enforcement bunch because on paper he owned practically nothing. Hell, I wouldn't have been all that surprised to learn that he managed to take advantage of the Earned Income Tax credit. But anyone who discounted Paddy O'Brien, in any way, did so at their own peril.

Within ten minutes I was pulling into the township of Longton, a tiny little enclave, just off the Interstate but sheltered by a wealth of woods. Longton has all of five roads, so if you have no clue where to find someone or something all you have to do is drive up and down all five, each about three blocks long, until you come across them. I'd been out here once before, for pleasure, not business. And even though it had been several years, it didn't take much time to pull into the circular drive of a three-story, plantation-looking home at the south end of the main drag.

Staggered along the length of the drive, both facing towards and away from the house itself, I saw a Lincoln, two 'Vettes and a Mercedes. Even with the Cherokee fairly new, I began to feel a bit outclassed.

I wondered if he had some sort of business meeting going on. If so, it would be damned smart to turn right around and head back.

Even as I thought of this, the front door opened and a man stepped outside and motioned me to a spot on the side of the driveway.

I pulled over as directed and sat with the motor idling and the tranny still in drive, ready to bolt if necessary. The guy, in his mid-twenties and wearing sport coat, slacks and open neck Oxford shirt, came over to my window.

"May I help you?" he asked.

Cultured tones, like he'd had some university time or something. I couldn't place the accent, but it didn't sound Midwestern to me.

And most definitely not Irish.

"I was wondering if it'd be possible for me to speak with Mr. O'Brien," I said.

The guy looked me over a bit, then stepped back and examined the Cherokee. It crossed my mind that he was looking to see if it was rigged to blow up or something.

"Is the boss expecting you?"

"I don't think so, but one never knows."

The fellow's composure slipped a bit at that, and now he looked kind of puzzled.

"Your name?"

"Sam Quinton."

He nodded but didn't give any sign that the name meant anything.

Probably not a wrestling fan.

"Just a second, Mr. Quinton."

The guy made a motion with his hand, and from somewhere around the corner stepped another guy who looked and dressed about the same.

Guy number one went into the house while number two took up a position about ten yards away from me. These two looked like soldiers, smooth and competent, and it seemed as if Paddy may have raised his employment standards since the last time I'd seen him.

It took barely thirty seconds before number one came out and waved me out of the Cherokee. I shifted into park, shut off the engine, and joined him on the porch steps.

"Mr. O'Brien will be glad to see you," he said as the second fellow disappeared somewhere around the side of the house, "but I'm sure you understand that I have to . . ."

He raised his hands, palms up about chest level.

Turning my back on him, I raised my arms above my head and let him go at it.

The fellow did a smooth, competent pat down. With my training and background, I could have had him on the ground with half his joints popped inside of three seconds.

Unless, that is, he was a lot more dangerous than he looked. Satisfied that I had no weapons on me, he ushered me in the house.

A few seconds later, I was once again in the presence of Paddy O'Brien, one of the most vicious, bloodthirsty gangsters in the Midwest, a man whose legend in Missouri, Kansas and Illinois rivaled that of Whitey Bulger in New England, the man who the FBI claimed had committed no less than thirty murders with his bare hands.

"Blondie!" Paddy cried as I walked into the room. He bounded out of his chair, rushed over, and clasped me in a bear-hug every bit as hard and intimidating as any I'd ever suffered in the ring. When he finally let me down, it felt as if at least a couple of ribs had cracked.

While I fought to breathe, I took stock of the room. We were in Paddy's office, a kind of smallish, cozy affair made up of a lot of dark brown wood and cracked leather chairs, the old-fashioned kind adorned with brass studs.

Besides myself and Paddy, half a dozen men lounged around the room. None of them what I'd expected. In the past, any time I'd seen Paddy a group of thick-necked, skinned-knuckle bruisers accompanied him. The kind of man who looked right at home in a bar filled with bikers or down by a pier somewhere knocking stevedores around.

But all of these men were younger, smoother, like the guy in the suit who'd greeted me at the door. These guys looked plain out of place in the office of a thug like O'Brien.

"What's up, fella?" Paddy asked when I'd got my breath back and we'd both sat down. "Why you been away from your number one so long?"

I took a moment to size Paddy up. It had been about five years since I'd last seen him, but he hadn't changed a whole lot. Six eight and at least three hundred pounds of muscle, including the most barrel-shaped chest I'd ever seen, he had to be coloring his hair. It for sure wasn't a rug, and nobody pushing sixty could have hair that reddish-black.

If so, the dye job probably extended to his beard as well. As long as I'd known him, you could spot Paddy's beard, reddish-gold in color, extending out inches from his face.

"You're right," I said, "it has been a while. I've been trying to earn a living, which isn't as easy as it should be. In fact, I really hate to say it but this isn't a social call."

"Oh?" A slight hooding effect swept over his eyes. Despite how much he may like a person, and Paddy had always proclaimed himself my number one fan from my ring days, at his core he was a shrewd, cautious criminal.

"Yeah, sorry Paddy."

"You wanting to sell me a membership to your gym in the city? Think I'm out of shape?"

He pounded his fist on his chest, causing a slight booming sound in the room.

"Hardly," I said, working to put a grin on my face. "No, this has to do with my other business."

That hooding over the eyes intensified.

"The private eye thing? You investigating me, Blondie?"

"Not at all," I said, "but I want to talk about something you may be able to help me with."

Paddy settled back with a faint smile on his face. "Shoot," he said.

With Paddy, direct's usually the only way to go.

"Do you know a girl named Tammy Dodger?"

Nobody sucked in their breath or ran panicked from the room. Nothing as dramatic as that. But sitting there watching Paddy, who appeared as calm as could be, I felt a definite tension among the men scattered around.

"Why you ask?"

"Because she was found murdered yesterday, and a client of mine was involved."

"Who's your client?"

I thought about that one for a second, then decided there would be no harm in saying. No more harm could come to

Nicky, of course, and if Paddy had nothing to do with the affair, I doubted if the name would mean anything.

On the other hand, if Paddy had ordered the girl, or Nicky or both of them killed, I stood a good chance of not walking out of the house.

"His name's Nicky LeBow."

Paddy's face scrunched up.

"LeBow? That sounds kind of familiar."

He looked to a man standing off to his right.

"Do we know this Tammy what's her name?"

The guy furrowed his brow for a second.

"I think she works at Dorsey's. That the one you mean?"

I nodded.

"And you say your client killed her?" Paddy asked.

I noticed a couple of his men tense across the shoulders.

I shook my head, beginning to feel a worm of fear. Paddy hadn't survived as long as he had by misunderstanding what people around him were saying.

"No, Paddy. I said my client was involved, but I'm not exactly sure how, and I may never know."

Paddy raised his eyebrows. If he was acting, he was doing one hell of a job.

"Why's that?"

"Because," I said, looking him straight in the eye, "sometime last night or early this morning someone killed him. Shot him three times and left him behind a building at the university."

Everyone in the room stared at me without blinking. I could actually hear a couple of indrawn breaths, and the atmosphere seemed to coagulate around me. I kept my gaze level with Paddy's while at the same time trying to track the other men in the room with my peripheral vision.

But considering that I didn't have any kind of weapon with me, I didn't really see what I could hope to accomplish.

Then I figured, what the hell, and lobbed another grenade into the middle of all that.

"What about a doctor named Richards?"

I distinctly heard a sip of air from at least one of the men behind me. Paddy, though, appeared as unperturbed as ever.

"Richards?" he asked. "Don't think I know the man. What kind of doctor is he?"

"Podiatrist, from what I hear."

"You mean he works on feet?"

I nodded.

"He's been out of the country for a few weeks, but the cops are expecting him back sometime today. It was his house that the girl was found dead in."

"Blondie, Blondie. I haven't seen you in years, then you show up asking about a dancer, some old foot doctor and a two-bit gambler? What are you expecting out of me?"

I could still feel all that tension, but some of the men within eyesight had relaxed a little. I guessed Paddy's men were taking their cue from him, and he was definitely trying to smooze me. Which, I figured, was better than shooting me.

I spread my hands, putting on my "aw shucks" grin.

"Hey, Paddy, what can I say? The girl worked at Dorsey's, which made me think of you, so I had to check it out."

A long, slow moment ticked by as Paddy stared me down. Then he broke into a grin of his own and stood up.

"Understood, Blondie. Just sorry that you wasted your time like this. You have any idea the turnover in girls out there? And I'm only in the place about once a month."

"Yeah?" I said.

"Yeah. Usually just long enough to bust the manager's head to keep him from holding out on me. As for this LeBow guy," he spread his hands in the most innocent way imaginable. "But hey. Don't be a stranger, okay?"

I stood up and held out my hand. Paddy shook it, giving my arm a couple of extra pumps.

A minute later, I was out on the driveway and climbing into the Cherokee. It didn't escape my notice that one of the clean-cut clones walked behind me and stood there watching as I drove away.

I got out of there with two questions on my mind.

One, what happened to all the thuggish-looking bruisers that Paddy used to surround himself with?

And two, maybe more important, if Paddy and his people had never heard of Nicky, how did they know he was a low-life gambler?

CHAPTER NINE

My cell phone buzzed about three minutes out from Paddy's house. Digging it out of my jacket pocket, I turned it on.

"What the fuck do you think you're doing?" a harsh, jangly voice screeched at me.

"Hey, Phil," I said, "how's it going?"

"Don't give me your 'hey, Phil' bullshit. What are you doing out there at O'Brien's?" I had to play it careful here. On the one hand, I really didn't care much for Lt. Phil Kronberg, and really didn't give a flying you know what about what he thought.

On the other hand, he was Josh Nichols's commanding officer in the department and could make all kinds of grief for my buddy. And if he chose to he could play hell with my PI license.

So, there was that.

"I thought you were out of town," I said.

"Got back in this morning. You going to answer my question?"

"How did you know I was out at Paddy's?" I asked.

"Don't you imagine we have that scuz under surveillance? Especially when one of his employees ends up dead?"

I thought back over my drive up to Paddy's, and the drive away. I hadn't noticed anything even remotely resembling surveillance.

"Are you sure?" I asked Kronberg. "I was just there and I didn't see any ice cream trucks or florist vans."

"Give us some credit, Quinton. We've got a little more subtlety than you may think."

I considered telling Kronberg how impressed I was with the word "subtlety" but decided it wouldn't really get me anywhere.

"What can I do for you, Lieutenant?"

Attaboy, Sam. Nice and cool. We're all friends here.

"You can stay the hell away from O'Brien, his place of business or anything even remotely connected with this case. This is an active homicide, private, and you're not involved. So, take a walk."

"But I am involved. It was my client who got himself killed."

"No, Quinton, you're not. Like I said, this is an active case, two in fact. That means you butt out and the professionals take over. Got that?"

I could have argued with that one. My license from the state empowers me to investigate felonies, including homicide. But there's the spirit of law and letter of law, and I had no doubt that if he wanted to Kronberg could find, or manufacture, some violation or other on my part.

"Got it, Lieutenant. You guys have a good time. And call me if you need any advice, okay?"

There was kind of a snap in my ear. Kronberg was the only person I'd ever known who could make turning off a smart phone sound like he'd slammed it down. I threw my phone on the driver's seat and continued down the Interstate back to Providence.

It had been an interesting little interlude in my week, but Kronberg, despite his gruffness, was right. Even if the cops weren't screaming at me, the last thing I wanted was to mess around in anything involving O'Brien. I was more than willing to take a few minutes to check things out with him, but beyond that I really didn't want to go.

Time for me to go back to earning an honest living. I had flab to burn off, books to balance and equipment to shine.

Unfortunately, though I didn't know it yet, I wasn't out of the thing just yet.

A sixty-year-old housewife was about to plunge me right back in.

CHAPTER TEN

The next morning, shortly before noon, I was at the gym plugging away at the heavy bag.

Bag work had never been a major part of my workouts as a pro wrestler, mainly because while the punches and slaps in wrestling do make contact, they land without a whole lot of impact. But as I was getting on in years and finding it harder and harder to keep the Bomber's legendary waistline, I'd found that heavy bag work did a lot for my heart rate, which in turn helps out some with the waistline.

I had the bag set up in the corner, where the thwacking as I hit it back and forth wouldn't be as bothersome for the clients in the main part of the gym.

"Yo, Sam," Lisa called out from across the room.

I looked up to see her standing in the office doorway, next to a nicely-dressed older woman.

I grabbed the bag with my left hand, slowing its oscillations until it came to a stop.

Then, grabbing a sweat towel from a bench propped in the corner, I headed towards the office.

"What's up?" I asked as I approached Lisa and the older woman.

"New client to see you."

I shrugged.

"No offense, ma'am, but Lisa can take care of you as well as I could."

"Not a gym client, Sam," Lisa said.

I took a step back and gave the lady the once over. Although I'd pegged her from across the gym as early sixties, I realized now that I could be off five years or so either way. Medium height, and looking in decent shape, despite the silver hair and a slight stoop to the shoulders, she only had a smattering of wrinkles and a fairly straight posture.

She was wearing a simple navy dress, no frills or pattern at all, but I had a sneaking hunch that the garment cost about as much as the monthly insurance I paid for the gym.

"Sam Quinton," I said, holding out my slightly-sweaty hand.

The woman took it, managed not to grimace or sneer, and smiled at me in return.

"Lucy Richards," she said.

I got it in about a second, then gave her a closer inspection.

"Richards," I said.

She smiled, though with quite a bit of stress in her face.

"Yes," she said, "as in the wife of Dr. Bill Richards. I assume that's what you were thinking?"

I nodded. Lisa had eased her way off. Out of the corner of my eye, I saw her explaining to a girl with pipe-stem arms how to do curls with three-pound weights.

I gave my face another pass with the towel and ushered Mrs. Richards into my office.

She gave the place a once over, expressing neither despair nor elation. I saw her eyes light on the Belt, but while she frowned for a moment, she moved on and focused on one of the empty chairs set in front of my desk.

I motioned to the chair, and she sat without another look at the Belt.

Another non-fan.

"How may I help you, Mrs. Richards?"

She took a moment to smooth her dress over the tops of her thighs.

"My husband and I arrived back from Orleans, France late last night," she said.

I nodded.

"And of course, we were met by the police. As arranged, seeing as how they called us back early."

I nodded again. Duke Prowder, who got me into this business, always stressed that when you've got them talking, don't get in the way. Duke worked almost his entire life as a detective and was nice enough in his golden years to take me on and show me the ropes, so I'd done my best to soak up every bit of wisdom he had.

"As you can imagine, Mr. Quinton, this is a rather distressing situation."

"I'm sure," I said.

"Finding out that someone was hiding out in our home while we were gone is bad enough. I believe the man in question was a friend of yours."

Friend was a bit of a stretch when describing Nicky, but I let it go with my third nod of the morning.

"But I probably could have accepted that. Have you lived in Providence long, Mr. Quinton?"

"Sam. And I was born here, but for a long time I lived away."

"How long have you been back?"

"Around five years or so," I said.

"Then you've no doubt seen some changes around here since you were younger, right?"

I grinned, remembering Nichols's comment from the other day.

"It ain't Mayberry anymore," I said.

She grinned a bit in return, though the strain didn't leave her face.

"So true. And that was never more apparent to me than when we came home to the news of a girl murdered in our house."

I decided to take a shot at something.

"A girl who you and your husband didn't know," I said.

She hesitated, just for a second. Barely noticeable, but it was there. "Yes," she replied. "A girl who I didn't know."

This woman was sharp, and I had the feeling that she'd noticed the little snare I'd set and had willingly walked into it.

"What can I do for you, Mrs. Richards?"

"As I said, the police informed us that the young man who was—inhabiting—our house was a friend of yours."

"More like an acquaintance. He came to me when he found the girl and asked me to smooth things over with the cops."

She nodded, as if I'd passed some sort of test.

"Rather an unusual request to make of a health club owner, isn't it?"

I smiled at her, mainly to hide my grimace at the description of my place as a "health club."

"That's just one of my businesses."

"Ah yes." Lucy Richards smoothed her dress over her thighs again, though I couldn't see a single wrinkle.

"I believe Sgt. Nichols said something about you being a private detective."

"That's me," I said, keeping the smile in place and wondering just when she would get to the point.

"Quite a leap from being a professional wrestler to that, isn't it? Owning a gym I can understand, but . . ."

I shrugged.

"I started wrestling my last year in high school. Wanted to go straight into it after school, but mom insisted on at least trying college. Which I did, but only for a couple of years. Earned some recognition for my athletics but didn't really take to the school part. So, I dropped out and got into pro wrestling. For the first two years, when peanuts were being thrown my way, I worked on a loading dock during the week."

"Did you ever make a career of it?" Lucy Richards asked.

"I was lucky enough to go pro, but for a second-rate federation. I got a shot at the big time once, but by then I was getting up there in age. So, I never really developed much of a career skill set. Unfortunately, a few years ago I tore my knee pretty bad and had to give it up."

"Then how did you . . ."

I shrugged again. If I kept talking to her much longer, my shoulders would have a nice workout.

"Up until the time I hurt my knee, I'd never given much of a thought to anything other than the ring. I had no marketable skills, but I look strong and imposing, so I started working as a bouncer for a few of the clubs in St. Louis. One night a man named Bill Prowder came in. He was a PI staking out a client's husband for a divorce case. He saw me handle a couple of loud mouths, nothing really out of the ordinary, but I guess he liked what he saw. Bill, everyone called him Duke, was getting on in years and couldn't really handle the rough stuff anymore, not that there's that much involved, but you never know when it will pop up. I thought it over for a bit, then went to work for him."

"And from there you moved back home and started your own agency?"

I nodded.

"After I filled out all the requisite forms and paid the state licensing fees."

"And this gym?"

"Mrs. Richards," I said, "why don't we get to why you're really here?"

For the first time since entering my office, she broke eye contact. Looking away, her gaze darted to the four corners before coming back to me.

When it did, I saw the beginning of a red puffiness around her eyes, and the tension in her face had jumped up a couple of notches.

"I want you to investigate my husband," she said, her voice softer than before and cracking on the last syllable.

I stayed quiet, almost positive there was more.

"I believe he knew the girl they found in our home."

I breathed deep, maintaining my silence.

"And I think he knows why she—and your friend—were killed."

CHAPTER ELEVEN

"It began about six months ago," Mrs. Richards said.

I'd gotten her a soda out of the mini fridge next to my desk, settled on water for myself, then eased back into my chair to hear her story.

"My husband's been retired for a little over a year. At seventy, he finally decided to hang it up. The kids were both grown long ago, of course, and we've got more than a few grandchildren, so after being consumed by first med school and then his practice for nearly forty years, Bill decided it was time to relax."

"But I'm guessing he didn't relax as much as you'd hoped?" I asked.

She shook her head, and again a slight puffiness appeared around her eyes. I cringed at the thought of how much raw emotion she was battling to contain within herself.

"There were—odd—phone calls. Sometimes coming at all hours. At first, Bill shrugged them off as former patients needing treatment, but I'm not that naive."

"Hard to imagine a foot emergency at midnight," I said.

She nodded, and a grin broke through, briefly, from her obvious pain.

"Exactly."

"Was there some commonality to the calls?" I asked.

She gave me a puzzled frown.

"I mean were they the same caller? Different ones? Male or female? Ages?"

"Almost all men, at least, the ones that I answered. And even though they were different voices, they all sounded the same."

"The same how?"

She made a vague waving motion with her hands.

"I guess you'd say, kind of flat. But cultured at the same time."

The image of all those preppy types that had been hanging around Paddy's house flitted through my head.

"And it was as this was going on that Bill began to change."

I brought myself back to the here and now.

"Change how?"

"His appetite seemed to leave him. He began to jump at the most ordinary sounds. One time, I came up behind him, he was sitting on the couch, and leaned over to plant a kiss on his cheek. As soon as my hair brushed his face he jumped up and whirled around, as if I were attacking him."

The tension had now moved down to her shoulders and arms. The lady was holding herself as straight as possible, as if at the slightest motion she would crumble into a heap.

I was starting to get a picture myself. A rather abstract one, but it was slowly coming together.

"Mrs. Richards," I said, "why were you and your husband in France for the last few weeks?"

"I suggested a trip, but somewhere in the States. I just wanted to try to get away and see if Bill would relax a bit."

"Did he want to go?"

"Not at first. I spent a few months nagging him, but he kept coming up with excuses. Then, week before last, he suddenly decided he wanted to go and suggested Europe. I thought that was a bit extreme, but was just relieved that he'd relented, so I went along."

"And you were going to be gone a month?"

"Correct. But that obviously got cut short when the police contacted us. How long was your friend staying in our house?"

I considered correcting her again as to my status vis-a-vis LeBow. When we'd first entered the office, I really hadn't cared much what she thought of me. But in the last few minutes I'd begun to develop an admiration for this woman.

However, she had more important things on her mind than my feelings.

"He'd been staying there about that length of time. For what it's worth, he usually left homes in the same, or better, condition than he found them. And I never knew him to rip off the places he stayed at."

"No, he just left dead bodies lying around." She paused, took a deep breath and squared her shoulders. "I'm sorry Mr. Quinton – Sam. I shouldn't take my feelings out on you."

"Ma'am, what exactly is it you want me to do?"

"I want to hire you to get to the bottom of all this. I thought that was clear."

"Well, you see, there's a problem. It's an active police case now. A double homicide at that."

"And you can't be involved?"

"I can be, but there's nothing I can do that they can't. Believe me, they're taking the whole thing seriously, and all I can see doing would be to get in their way."

I didn't know if she'd buy it, but figured it sounded better than explaining that Kronberg had warned me off.

She furrowed her brow for a moment.

"Okay, how about this. I don't hire you to investigate the dead girl. Just to find out what's going on with my husband."

I mulled that one over. It wasn't exactly ironclad, but it would at least get me a foot in the door, and I was feeling a bit guilty over Nicky.

"Okay, Mrs. Richards. If you want to, I'll check out your husband. You suspect he may have known the dead girl?"

She hesitated, and for the first time a trace of doubt flickered across her face.

"I probably shouldn't have said it like that," she said, "but I believe that something's going on with him that he won't share.

After all, what possible reason could someone have to kill her and leave her in our house? It just doesn't make any sense."

"And all of these odd phone calls have taken place in the last half year or so?" I asked.

She paused again, this time worry lines appearing on her face.

"There have been—other—incidents in the past. Odd phone calls, nights when he'd call at the last minute and say he'd be late getting home. But I guess I just played the faithful wife and dismissed them."

"Going back how far?"

"I'm not sure," Mrs. Richards replied. "But easily years. With raising the kids, I guess I just learned to turn a deaf ear."

I drummed my fingers on the desk, trying to put it all together.

"How much do you charge?" she asked a moment later.

I quoted my daily rate, and the lady scored another point with me when she didn't flinch or try to haggle me down. Without another word, she got out her checkbook.

"How much do you need to start?"

CHAPTER TWELVE

Shortly after Lucy Richards and I had concluded our business, she left the gym and I followed not too far behind. I stopped first and left a few instructions with Lisa, then stepped outside and climbed into my car, tossing my cell on the passenger seat and pulling out of the parking lot before heading north on Arena Avenue. Sure enough, a couple of heartbeats afterwards a grungy, dust-covered blue Datsun pulled out into my lane and began trailing me. Noticing the state of the car, I thought maybe I'd overreacted.

Either that, or organized crime was even more on life support than most people imagined.

From the strip mall, if you stay north on Arena you're out of the city in no time at all. Barely three minutes saw me entering a wooded, hilly area where the road began to curve and dip. For the moment, I was still technically within Providence city limits, but the various habitations, mainly isolated houses and convenience stores, became few and far between.

A glance in the mirror showed the blue Datsun still behind me.

Didn't mean anything in itself, but my antenna, at half mast earlier, was steadily straightening towards full attention.

I decided to verify my hunch.

A forty-five-degree curve was coming up, with an eighty-year old church right past the bend of the curve. About forty feet out, I floored the accelerator and, after a second's hesitation, the Cherokee responded.

Praying that no vehicle lurked around the bend, I whipped through the curve and into the church parking lot, deserted at this time of day. Once in the parking lot I did a quick modified bootlegger's turn, not an easy feat in my vehicle, and ended up facing out, my heart steadying down as the seconds ticked by.

If whoever was in the Datsun had been following me, they surely had seen me deliberately speeding up to escape. I was just hoping that they thought that's all I was trying to do.

My cell phone chirped. I let it go because, if my ploy worked, I wanted both hands on the wheel.

In the next breath, the blue Datsun came roaring around the curve, the thuggish-looking driver hunched over the wheel. As he passed the church lot, his head whipped my way. But even though he saw me he didn't have time to course correct before shooting down the road.

I pulled out right behind him, and when it came to negotiating country roads, it took no time at all for the Cherokee to force him off the road and into a tree. I switched off the ignition, threw the keys on the seat next to my phone and bounded out of my vehicle.

The guy was tough, for sure. By the time I got there, he was climbing out of the Datsun, shaking his head and rubbing his hand across his face.

When he saw me coming his way, he set himself, and I could tell by his stance that he'd been in a scrap or two in his life. But he was still a bit groggy from meeting up with the tree, and I was as alert as I'd been in I didn't know how long.

The thug threw a right my way. If it had come in straight, it would have taken my head off, but he threw it in a kind of loop, which allowed me to duck under and inside, ending in a modified squat, and I used that move to rocket my own right up into his solar plexus.

"Uggh," came out of his mouth as he staggered about a foot back. But he didn't go down and set himself again.

By that time, though, I'd covered the distance between us and threw my shoulder into his chest, driving him back against the wrecked mess of his car. A forearm across the throat kept him stationary while I pounded another short, hard jab into the solar.

Then I stepped back and let Tough Guy slump to the ground.

I stood there and let him gag and hack, waiting for him to get a little coherence back.

Tall, as tall as me, and with a hefty pair of shoulders and chest. But this guy hadn't been frequenting my gym, or any other, for a while. His gut didn't exactly hang over his belt, but it was the kind of hard fat that bulged out in front and the sides.

Even so, fat is fat, and it'll slow you down when you need to move.

Toughie's face looked like it had been broken a time or two, and the last time not set as carefully as it could have been. He had most of his hair, for his age, but a lot had departed from the hairline, and he wore what remained a little too long on the sides.

"Damn," he finally wheezed out, "you hit hard."

I shrugged and gave him the Blond Bomber "aw shucks" grin. "Maybe," I said, "or maybe you're softer than you should be."

"Yeah," he replied as he struggled up to his knees, "I wouldn't be surprised."

"Do I know you?" I asked.

"Maybe, maybe not. I've been around for a while."

By now he'd managed to stand all the way up even though his knees wobbled a bit. "I always thought you wrestler types were a bunch of phony actors."

"We are," I said. "But some of us came up the hard way. Those who are actually tough can sell the make believe that much better."

The bruiser shook his head, then groaned and placed his right hand alongside of it.

"I probably shouldn't have done that," he said as a light finally clicked on in my own head.

"Rogan," I said.

He nodded, gingerly. "That's me," he said, "Sean Rogan."

"You're one of Paddy's guys."

A new dullness showed up in his eyes and his head ducked down a bit.

"I used to be," he said, "not so much anymore."

That one puzzled me. Paddy O'Brien was famous for his loyalty to his workers. Even those who sometimes made mistakes were always given second or third chances. Lots of his guys were originally from the old country, had found their way across the water and to the East Coast, then eventually meandered across the country to end up in the Midwest, where Paddy gave them good jobs and good incomes.

At the same time, I remembered how confused I'd been on my recent visit to his house when I saw all those smooth, business types he had around him.

"You mean he fired you?" I asked.

Rogan nodded, and this time his head didn't seem to bother him as much.

"About six months ago. Me and most of the other guys. About the same time those pretty boys showed up."

I wanted to laugh. I hadn't heard the phrase "pretty boy" since the eighties. Rogan said it with utmost seriousness.

"So why were you following me, Sean?"

He spread his hands.

"Some of the guys are keeping tabs on the boss. Trying to figure out what the hell's going on. I heard you were up there yesterday to talk to him, so I thought maybe I'd shag you around and see what came up."

It sounded reasonable, if a bit lunkheaded. But his explanation still left one little piece dangling.

"What about yesterday morning? At the university? That was you there as well, right? At the crime scene? You weren't on me then, right? So, what's the deal?"

A whole bunch of emotions flitted across Rogan's face. His expression went through about twenty different convulsions before they settled on what he probably figured passed for open-faced honesty.

"I got a call," he finally said.

"A call?"

"Yeah, from one of Paddy's other guys. Or former guys."

"Okay," I said, "I'm getting lost as all hell here. What is it you're trying to do?"

The Irish lug sighed, and for a moment his eyes crossed.

Probably trying to think.

"Look," he finally said, "I'm going to trust you. Paddy always talked good about you, from back when you were in the ring and all."

"Okay."

"So why don't I give you the short version, and if you want we can go somewhere and talk it over in more detail?"

I nodded, more confused now than when this whole show began.

"I think—that is, we all think—that Paddy's in trouble."

"Trouble?"

The guy nodded, and something like actual pain may have flickered behind those eyes.

"We think someone's taking him over."

Great, I thought. Just great. I set out to help a guy who comes into my gym. All I had to do was act as a simple intermediary between him and the cops.

Then I end up getting hired by a scared old lady to find out her husband's secret.

And now, it seems, I was tiptoeing around the edge of an all-out mob war.

CHAPTER THIRTEEN

A little over an hour later, Rogan and I walked out of a small bar on the county outskirts and shook hands. I offered him a ride into town, but he'd called a friend of his who was coming to pick him up.

I frowned at that. Over beer, he hadn't been able to tell me a whole lot, but what he had said was troubling, to say the least.

"It began about six months back. There wasn't any big shakeup or anything, no meeting as such. But every week one or two of us old timers were let go, Paddy telling us times had changed and he didn't need us anymore."

Six months again. The same time frame as when Mrs. Richards noticed a change in her husband.

"Didn't need any help?" I asked.

"Naw, not that. Because this was about the same time that those smooth guys, what some of us call the clones, began showing up. Bit by bit they began taking over all of our duties, leaving us old guys standing around with our thumbs up our asses."

"The clones?"

"You were out at Paddy's yesterday, right?"

"Uh huh."

"You surely saw them. Those college-boy looking guys. With their blazers and ties and tailored holsters to hold their pansy Berettas. As we were put out to pasture, they came on board."

"Where'd all the old guys go?"

Rogan shrugged.

"Some went to KC. Others to St. Louis. I heard from one or two of them who ended up down in New Orleans for a while."

In a weird, offbeat way, it sounded kind of sad. The men Rogan referred to, including himself, were probably all stone-cold killers, the kind who would slit their brother's throat if the boss said so. Sure, they probably spent most of their lives hiding behind a placard of Irish pride and Old Country blood and guts, but when it came right down to it they were all thugs, pure and simple.

Yet such a life didn't come with much of a retirement plan, and most guys like this wouldn't know a mutual fund if it smacked them in the face. Cut off from their boss, they were like undirected children, wandering the landscape and searching for a home that wasn't there anymore.

This didn't sound like the Paddy O'Brien that I'd known for years. It didn't sound like him at all.

Beyond the basic situation, though, Rogan didn't have a whole lot to offer me. He did point out that, as the old guys faded away and the "clones" kept showing up, Paddy's movements became more and more restricted.

For the moment, I pretty much shrugged that off as the sour grapes of an ex-employee. When I asked him about Nicky, or the girl killed at the doctor's house, or even Dr. and Mrs. Richards, he professed no knowledge of any of it.

And for the first time I didn't quite believe him. As soon as I'd mentioned Richards, something had flitted through Rogan's eyes. I tried going at it a couple of different ways but couldn't budge him at all.

Didn't know anything about Nicky or Tammy Dodger or Doc Richards. I believed him on the first two but not the third.

After failing to budge him I gave up on it, at least for a while.

"I think I'll head out to Chicago for a few weeks," he said as we went outside and waited for his friend to show up. "Try to lay low until we see how this thing works out."

His cavalier attitude made me wonder if Paddy was really in as much trouble as Rogan had claimed, or if I was being played in some way. It was his life and his call, and for all I knew a lifetime working as a mob tough had left him worn down and, maybe, a little frightened.

So, I left him and headed over to my Cherokee. As I climbed in, my cell phone, still resting on the passenger seat, chirped.

I realized then that, after that whole deliberate business with having Lisa start a chain of calls for me, I'd never gotten around to calling Nichols back.

I turned the phone on as I began backing out of the bar's parking lot.

"Where the hell've you been?" Nichols barked at me in greeting.

"Nice to talk to you, too," I said. "I'm fine, by the way. Just in case you were wondering."

"I was wondering. At first. After a half hour or so I decided to start earning my taxpayer-provided salary and stop worrying about you. What was all that song and dance with Lisa calling me, anyway?"

"Just a contingency that it turned out I didn't need. So thanks, but I've got it handled."

There was a long pause on my buddy's end before he spoke up.

"Sam," he said, "you're keeping clear of O'Brien, right? And this whole mess with LeBow?"

"Of course," I said, "as your boss so rightly pointed out to me, you guys have got it more than handled. Too bad, though. If real life were more like TV, it would be more fun."

"And a hell of a lot more dangerous. But what do you know about real life? You spent most of your adult time playacting in spandex tights."

"Yeah, but I'm all grown up now. Speaking of which, I've got grown up stuff to do, so I'd better sign off."

"You're staying clear of all this, right?" Nichols repeated. "Even as wild as Providence has gotten the last few years, two murders in two days is a bit much. But we've got it under control. Okay?"

"Jeez, Josh, okay. I get it. You guys are on the job, and I've got my gym to run. 'Nuff said."

I hung up and turned my full concentration back to my driving. As the highway curved, turning into Arena Avenue right at the city limits, I replayed in my mind everything that Rogan had told me.

I didn't yet know how Paddy's situation fit in with the Richards's, if indeed it did. But if it didn't, then there was a whole lot of coincidence flying around. And as Duke Prowder had taught me when I was learning the business, coincidence is a fancy word for something not yet understood.

CHAPTER FOURTEEN

The next morning, I waited at the gym until Lisa showed up. When she did, I traded keys with her and, explaining that I needed something a little lower profile than the Cherokee, pulled out of the parking lot in her 2008 gray Focus.

The Cherokee may be fun to drive, but it's not the best plan to attempt a surreptitious tail while wheeling around in it.

Shortly before nine, I pulled up and parked about three blocks down from Paddy's house.

Even in the Focus, I felt way too conspicuous in a village the size of Longton. The entire town probably didn't have more than fifty cars, and here I was sitting idle on the same street as one of the most notorious mobsters in the Midwest.

I was banking on the hope that something would cause me to be moving before too long, otherwise sooner or later I'd look up in my rear-view mirror and see a deputy sheriff pulling in behind me.

This was the kind of situation where I regretted my physical appearance. When shadowing or tailing someone, the ideal is to be as inconspicuous as possible. Despite the usual public perception, most of your really successful PI's, even bodyguards for that matter, look like accountants or store managers.

When you're six three, and weighing well over two hundred pounds of mainly, even at my age, muscle and have long blond hair that you never could quite bring yourself to cut off, blending into the crowd is almost impossible.

What I needed, I thought as I cracked open a thermos of coffee and poured myself a cup, was to look like Paddy's new employees. The "clones," as Rogan had called them, all looked like they'd come off the assembly line at an MBA school. But despite their soft appearance and dress, I had a hunch that I shouldn't underestimate them.

Some of the most dangerous men I've ever met looked at first glance like they'd cry if you spit at them.

A few minutes in, I saw a vehicle pulling out of Paddy's parking lot. I'd parked facing south, which meant that anyone leaving would have to go past me to get to the highway. As the car, a modest, light blue Mercedes, came alongside of me, I raised the coffee cup to take a drink.

I made the gesture as natural as possible, hoping that it would obscure enough of my face that I wouldn't be recognized. Providing, of course, that the Mercedes's occupant had seen me the day before.

The motion of drinking obscured part of my vision, but I saw enough to spot the driver as one of Rogan's clones, but I couldn't make out if he'd been one of the ones I'd encountered on my first trip out here.

Tracking the car in my rear-view mirror, I waited till he was almost to the turnoff to the highway before starting up my own car and turning to go after him.

Staying unobserved wasn't that hard for a while. The same hills and dips in central Missouri that provide cover for a host of meth labs also make it easy to hang back far enough to avoid being seen by the car ahead. And since the county highways around the area don't have a whole lot of turnoffs, once someone starts down them it's easy to guess where they're headed.

Even without all of that, I had a fifty-fifty chance of figuring the guy's general direction.

Within ten minutes, the interstate came within view, but at the same time the landscape leveled out a bit, so I had to slow down and stay back even more. Not much of a problem, because odds were he was going to exit east and head towards Providence. Though there was a chance he'd take the west exit and scoot towards Kansas City.

I was banking on the shorter, more practical direction, and I was right.

With the interstate looming upon us, we both took the exit within about fifty feet of each other. At this point, I wasn't all that worried if he spotted me. A car coming behind him from the south would have had to stay behind him all the way, and it was more likely than not that such a car would be headed, as he was, towards Providence. There simply weren't any other cities around of any size, so at this point it would seem natural and obvious for both of us to be heading the same direction.

Of course, there was the slight possibility that he was heading towards St. Louis, about a hundred miles past in the same direction. Or any one of the numerous smaller towns between here and there. If so, I'd just have to do my best to keep track of him for the long stretch.

The trick would come when he departed the interstate, as I assumed he would, and ended up in the city. Lisa's car was plain enough that it would be a cinch to go unobserved by the average person, but if my quarry was any kind of a pro, he would spot me at some point, even if tangentially, and remember the car down the line.

As the exit for Arena Avenue came up and he turned on his blinker, I began to breathe a little easier.

Duke Prowder had taught me well, and I managed to wend my way through Providence's downtown area without losing the guy and, I thought, without him spotting me.

Eventually, we headed east again, out of downtown, and ended up on the outskirts of town. A few minutes later, and he was pulling into his destination.

Monty's Cues.

Monty's, situated just on the eastern edge of town at the end of a strip mall, served as Providence's premier pool joint. True, there were a couple of pool places downtown close to the university, but those were largely frequented by students. For the serious player, Monty's was the place to go.

The strip mall also held a donut shop. A quick trip inside provided me with a dozen assorted donuts, in mid-morning almost their entire stock, to while away the time.

If I looked like I was grabbing a late morning snack, maybe I'd be that much more obscure. Settling down in the driver's seat of Lisa's car, I angled the mirror to give me a full sight view of Monty's, then sat back and watched to see what happened.

It was too early for them to be open, but a couple of lights barely visible through the blackened windows indicated someone was there.

I'd only made it through a chocolate cake donut and half of an old-fashioned when the clone came back out, slipping a small plastic bag into his jacket pocket. I only had a glimpse, from half a parking lot away, but I saw enough to guess what he had tucked away in the bag.

Was I following an old-fashioned bagman? I'd assumed that job description went out around the time of the Internet, but maybe I'd been wrong.

For the next hour or so we crisscrossed the city, stopping at a variety of bars, novelty shops and music stores that catered to students around town. Eventually, Clone Boy parked outside of a diner at the beginning of the lunch rush.

The eatery, paint peeling from the front and dirt crusted into the door, didn't look like the sort of place that would be the hub of some sort of criminal activity. I'd eaten in the place once or twice and found it passable, but I would never go out of my way to stop in there. I circled the block once and managed to parallel park about half a block down from his car.

Far as that went, he could have just stopped in for lunch. If so, I wished his intestines well.

I couldn't see Clone Boy from my vantage point, but I did have a good sight of his car. Of course, he could have caught my tail and slipped out the other side, but since I couldn't be in two places at once, I figured I'd just sit tight and see what transpired.

Turned out I didn't have to wait too long.

About ten minutes in, I caught a flash of blue out of my left peripheral vision, and a fist rapped on my window. I glanced up to see a man standing in the street next to my car.

I couldn't just drive away. I would have had to start the car, and parked cars sat both in front and behind me, so I would have had to wave him off and crimp my wheel in order to leave anyway, and something told me the guy wouldn't stand back and let me do that.

I considered flipping him off, in a display of my manhood, but as I glanced to my right I saw another fellow standing next to my passenger's side door, so I figured what the hell and did the smart thing.

I rolled my window down and gave the first man the Blond Bomber "aw shucks" grin.

"Out of the car, mister," the guy said.

First chance I got, I really had to work on getting the "aw shucks" back up to snuff.

I got out of the car, thinking of taking my jacket off and flexing my guns at him and his buddy, but when the one in front of me moved the flap of his blazer aside just far enough for me to see he had an actual gun, as opposed to my euphemistic ones, I relented on that as well.

All things considered I probably needed to rethink a lot of things.

The two men fronting me, doing it so smoothly that the people walking back and forth along the sidewalk wouldn't notice, were two more of the clones. About the same size, five ten or thereabouts, one was blond and the other brown-haired. They both wore blue blazers, tan slacks and white shirts.

At least their ties were different colors.

The one who'd shown me his weapon, the blond one, turned

his shoulder aside, a subtle cue to me to move away from the car and up onto the sidewalk. As I did so, Brown Hair moved back a step and a half to allow me to get onto the sidewalk.

Then they crowded me up against the passenger door, again doing it in such a way that most people wouldn't notice.

These guys were damned good.

'Course, I told myself, I could have probably broken them both in half without raising much of a sweat, but I decided to see where things would take themselves.

"What's the deal, fellas," I said, not bothering with the "aw shucks" this time.

"You've been following our friend. We want you to stop."

This came from Blond Guy, and as I turned his way, it occurred to me that I'd seen him the other day at Paddy's place. "Following?" I asked. "What do you mean? I was just thinking of having some lunch and you guys show up and . . ."

"Can it, Quinton. You came out to see Mr. O'Brien yesterday, and now you're following one of his employees around. You should think about stopping that."

Blond Guy then moved his blazer a tad and caressed the butt of his pistol. Again, so subtle that no one on the sidewalk but me would see it.

"Far as that goes," Brown Hair chimed in, "you may want to think about other people as well."

"Other people?"

Brown Hair nodded to his partner, who reached into his jacket and pulled out one of those little spiral notebooks. He flipped it open and began reading.

"Lisa Nolan. Female, divorced. Twenty-five years old, one brother who lives in Chicago. Mother is . . ."

"That's enough," I said, mentally kicking myself for being so stupid.

Obviously, the guy I'd been following had spotted me and called in the reserves. They'd spotted me and tagged the plate, which they'd somehow managed to run.

And since I'd borrowed Lisa's car, they now knew all they needed to know about her.

"Okay, fellas," I said, "message loud and clear. How about I go back to my gym and earn an honest living. Sound good?"

"In a minute," Brown Hair said. "Before you take off, tell us what exactly you're up to. I can't believe all this is for some no 'count gambling buddy of yours."

Were the situation not so serious, I'd be a little disconcerted at all the people the last few days who assumed Nicky LeBow and I were friends.

Assuming I got out of this in one piece maybe I should consider hanging out with a better class of people. "Look," I began, just as the original clone came out of the diner and walked up to us.

He had blond hair too, though his tan wasn't quite as intense. A blazer again, gray this time, along with black slacks and the requisite white shirt, but without a tie like the other two.

"Is it casual Thursday for you?" I asked, and before I could move, or even flinch, he zipped up to me and powered his right straight into my solar plexus.

Open handed, like a spear.

It hurt, of course, hurt like hell, and the short distance made the jab even more violent. I staggered, glad they'd already had me backed up against the car because it would have been humiliating to fall on my ass in the street.

I tried to keep my face composed and not show the hurt at the same time I struggled to get my breath back. Back in my ring days, I'd often been hit in the same spot by the edge of a steel chair, but then I'd always known the blow was coming and could set myself. And the guy wielding the chair had always pulled it at the last minute.

The three clones were grinning at me now, so maybe I didn't appear as nonchalant as I hoped.

Black spots danced at the edges of my vision.

"Listen up, Quinton," said Diner Boy. "You may think you're

a tough guy 'cause you used to prance around a wrestling ring in purple tights, but this is the real world. So, whatever you're up to, or think you're up to, why don't you go back to your boring little has-been life and stay out of the way of real men. Okay?"

"Actually, my tights were royal blue," I croaked.

"Whatever. Just don't let us catch you jerking around us, or Mr. O'Brien, again. You may think he's your buddy 'cause he used to hang out with you back in the old days, but he's not. He wants nothing to do with you. Got it?"

I nodded. "Got it," I said, the voice a little stronger this time.

"Then get the hell out of here. And don't forget, we can get to more people than just you."

I crawled around to the driver's side of Lisa's Focus, got in and after a few minutes managed to pull out into traffic. I drove away without once looking back at the three men, mentally gouging my eyes out at the stupidity of borrowing a friend's car.

At the same time, the Clones had made a mistake. At the very most, they had an hour or so from the time they spotted me to reciting all of Lisa's vital stats. Which could only mean one thing.

Whoever these guys were, they had access to resources that Paddy, on his best days, could never have dreamed of.

I breathed as deeply as I could, trying to keep the walls from closing on me.

CHAPTER FIFTEEN

After stopping to have a quick lunch and calm my jitters, I made my way back to the gym. Walking in, I noticed that Double H had shown up for his session with Lisa.

Harold Hammer had been coming to the gym three times a week since long before I'd owned it. Unfortunately, he was one of those genetic rarities who, no matter how much he worked out, would never put any muscle on, or even define that which he already had.

Around six feet tall, he reminded me a lot of that British comedian who had a show for one season on HBO a few years back. Tall and gangly, almost like a daddy longlegs, he had snow white hair, in his early forties, a thirteen-inch neck and probably six-inch biceps, if that.

Shortly after the former owner's death, when I discovered that he'd left the gym to me, one of the workers introduced me to Harold. He'd come across as sociable enough, except for a slight stutter that showed up when he became excited. When the worker introduced me as The Blond Bomber, Harold didn't show any recognition at all.

Such is fame.

The three of us had chatted for a while, before Harold went back to his workout. Seeing that he had the machine set on the absolute lowest possible setting, yet grunted and groaned as he attempted to lift the weight, I glanced at my new employee, who gave me a shrug as if to say "welcome to the business."

Now, some years later, Harold still worked out religiously three days a week although recently he'd begun doing longer and longer workouts. I suspected this was to spend as much time with Lisa as possible, yet he still hadn't put on even an ounce of new muscle.

As I passed by the two of them I waved. Harold, straining to lift the bar, that's right, just the bar, didn't notice me, but Lisa did. She mouthed "messages" as I waggled her keys.

Heading into the office, I grabbed a bottle of water from the mini fridge, then sat down at my desk. Square in the middle of the desk sat a small pile of message slips, held down by my car keys. I dropped Lisa's keys onto the surface, slipped mine into my jacket pocket, then began leafing through the slips.

Two were from salesmen I'd dealt with in the past who wanted to show me some new equipment. I set those aside to call later. Another was from a sports magazine that wanted me to call back about doing an interview of some sort. I fondled that one for a minute, considering.

Although the gray hairs told me it was time to grow up, being the Bomber had been a large part of my life and had given me a living, so to speak, for several years. It was no one's fault that I'd washed out after barely making the big time, but I'd still done well enough that every now and then I managed to cash in on my former popularity.

I set that message aside for a definite callback.

That left only one more pink slip, and this one made my stomach tighten up.

"PJ called. No message."

I stared at those four words. Who the hell was it from? I didn't know anybody with the initials PJ. I sat there for a while rummaging through my memory before the bulb above my head finally clicked on.

I only knew Paddy's middle name, James, because he'd mentioned it one night when we'd gotten sloshed at a St. Louis bar. I'd successfully defended the Belt that night (thanks to the show's writers), a few months before I injured my knee the first time. When he'd told me his middle name, he'd made me promise never to reveal it to anyone. Something about the name coming from one of his uncles, a man who he'd hated and despised his whole life.

So the PJ part of the message didn't cause a lot of concern, though I felt it kind of odd that he would use it. It was the "no message" part that made my abs contract.

Why not leave a message? If he went to the trouble of calling me at the gym, why not say what he wanted?

Only one possible answer, one that sent my thoughts further down the path they'd been on for a few hours now. I was beginning to believe that I had an inkling of what was going on with Paddy, and who, more or less, the Clone Boys were.

Or rather, who they represented.

But how any of this tied into Nicky LeBow, or the dead stripper, or the Richards's, I didn't yet have a handle on.

One thing for sure, though.

The Clone Boys may have warned me off, but it looked like I wasn't getting off the hook that easily.

CHAPTER SIXTEEN

I needed to check in with one of my clients, and hopefully her husband as well.

It was getting on to afternoon, so traffic downtown was a little thick. Fortunately, though, our downtown only covers about ten or so blocks east to west, so it wasn't like I had to negotiate Manhattan at rush hour.

The Trithorn, our newest hotel, sits square on the busiest part of Main Street. The nearest parking garage is several blocks away, but the builders took that into account, and behind the hotel they placed not only parking for guests but some overflow as well.

According to Mrs. Richards, she and her husband were staying here while their home was considered a crime scene. They had a suite several floors up, and this wasn't the sort of place that the city police department usually sprang to keep people in.

Which, of course, presented quite a question. Was the couple really that wealthy? I'm not an expert, but I found it hard to believe that a local physician would have made good enough to casually plunk down so much, especially since it would be up in the air just how long they'd be put out of their house.

And of course, I couldn't help but wonder if their seeming financial situation had anything to do with how a dead stripper ended up in their house.

Walking into the lobby and approaching the registration desk, I cinched my leather jacket up a little higher. Looking at all the jackets, ties and nice dresses moving to and fro around me, I felt kind of out of place.

Actually, the leather jacket was a little warm for inside the hotel, but I kept it on, hoping for some sort of visual effect when I braced the doctor.

* * *

The elevator let me out onto a carpeted hallway that felt totally silent. Beige colored walls and a spackled ceiling lent an air of solitude, and I guess that the people who stayed in the suites valued their privacy.

Almost as soon as I knocked on the door Lucy Richards opened it up. She smiled at me, but it was rather strained around the edges.

"Is your husband here?" I asked.

"Yes, he's taking a nap in the other room." She ushered me in and offered me a drink.

I turned her down and she got right down to business, keeping her voice just above a whisper.

"Have you found anything out, yet?"

"Nothing that I could say for sure, but I'm starting to have a few hunches. I've been mainly chasing my tail since you left yesterday, but I think I may have caught on to the fringe of something. And I think it's time I spoke with the doctor."

She tensed up, and I could only guess the forces running through this woman for the last several months.

"He's resting," she repeated. "Are you sure you need to . . ."

"Does he know anything about your hiring me?"

"Oh God, no."

"Good," I said in the same low tone. "Let's keep it that way. Go and get him, ma'am. It's important."

I'd stood outside the man's house and been employed by his

wife for a day or so now. A guy I knew had been murdered, I was pretty sure, because of something to do with the doctor.

But I hadn't yet laid eyes on him until he stumbled out of the back recesses of the suite. I'm not sure what I was expecting, but what I saw didn't even come close to my mental image.

Dr. William Richards looked so ordinary, except for the fact that he was almost colorless. Average height, average weight, at least for his age. His eyes a watery blue and his skin almost corpse like in its paleness. His hair was gray, not a dignified silver, and it hung lank and limp on the sides of his head. The only real color in the man were the dark charcoal smudges under his eyes.

"Who are you?" were his first words to me, said with a tired resignation.

"My name's Sam Quinton, Doctor Richards. I'm a private investigator."

He stared at me for a minute, then shuffled over to a white leather couch that spanned one wall of the room and sat down.

"I'm not sure why my wife let you in. But seeing as you're here, what can we do for you?"

I took a deep breath, framing my words as I did so.

"I'm looking into the deaths of Tammy Dodger and Nicky LeBow."

"Who?" the doctor asked, in what I figured for a stalling tactic.

"The woman found dead in your house and the man who found her."

"You mean the man who killed her?" Richards replied, his voice raising a bit.

"That's up for debate, sir. At any rate, I'm checking into their deaths and I've got a few questions for you."

He stared at me for a moment, then leaned forward and clasped his hands in front of him. Mrs. Richards had moved off to the side.

"I don't have much experience at this sort of thing," Dr.

Richards said, "but I find it hard to believe the law allows private citizens to mess around in murders. And I can't imagine who would have hired you."

The guy was sharp, and not too far off the mark.

"I can't talk about who hired me. We've got the same sort of confidentiality thing your profession has. But I am doing this kind of on the down low."

Richards stood up now, a hint of red coming into his face. "I really don't see equating the medical profession with your line of work," he said. "As far as that goes, you look more like a hood than anything else."

"Have much experience around hoods, doc?"

It was an idle shot, and I really didn't know what to expect from it, but the words definitely got some kind of reaction.

Richards went pale again, before flaming damned near crimson. His eyes narrowed, and if this had been a cartoon you could have seen the steam coming out from his ears.

"I don't know what you mean by that, young man, but I really don't think we have anything to say to each other, and I really don't think I need to answer any questions of yours."

"From what I heard, you told the police that you didn't know Miss Dodger, the young lady murdered in your house. Is that true?"

"Of course it is. I never met her, and for damned sure wouldn't let a woman like that in my home."

"A woman like what?"

"Come on, Mr. Quinton. Don't insult my intelligence. The police clued us in on what that girl did for a living."

"Well, maybe not on a social level then. Was she possibly a patient of yours?"

"I usually deal with older patients, of course. Somebody that young wouldn't have any use for my services. And what does any of that have to do with anything anyway? The cops got the person who did it. Even if they did let him out, just to get killed."

I had him going now. I'd stumbled on the tactic of making him think he was above me socially, and the guy just couldn't help but show the dumb thug how smart he was.

"Come on, doctor. No one downtown believes LeBow killed her. And whoever did didn't just pull your name out of a hat. There had to be some reason your house was picked to drop her body in."

The red heightened in his face. Mrs. Richards had faded all the way into the background, and now it was just me facing off against a geriatric retired foot doctor.

"I resent your implication, young man. My best guess would be that it was that lowlife, whatever his name was, who broke into our house. He's much more likely to associate with people like that than either myself or my wife."

"If you didn't know her, or the man, why are you hiding out here?"

"We're not hiding out, as you call it. The police still have our house marked as a crime scene, thanks to the sort of people you run with, and we can't go home."

"Maybe, but . . ."

"But nothing. I want you to leave now. As far as I can see you've got no legal standing in this matter. So, either you leave now or I'll call the police and have you escorted away. Don't think I won't press charges."

Try as I might, I couldn't possibly think of what sort of charges he could press against me. But it really didn't matter because, in a way, I'd gotten what I came for.

"Fair enough," I said. "I hope you understand I'm just trying to clear a guy's name. Far as I know, an innocent guy."

"If he's so innocent, how come he ended up murdered himself? The whole thing hangs a stink over my family, and who knows how long before we live it down. So just go now and leave us alone."

I nodded to Mrs. Richards, hung my head in what I hoped would pass for shame, and got out of there.

In the hall and walking towards the elevator, I thought of calling Nichols and relaying what had just taken place, then realized I really didn't have anything more to give him than a distinctly guilty vibe from the doc.

At the moment, that was more than enough.

CHAPTER SEVENTEEN

Since I couldn't go to the scene of the crime, so to speak, I decided to hit it from the other angle and drop by Dorsey's.

Dorsey's is your traditional type of gentleman's club. Located on an industrial stretch of road that runs through the middle of town, it sits on a street corner, complete with blacked-out windows and a small, inconspicuous sign. Basically, if you aren't looking for Dorsey's you'd never know it was there.

That may seem like an odd approach for a guy's place in a college town, complete with liquor, dancers and anything else one could imagine, but it was actually sound marketing strategy.

When it comes right down to it, college kids don't spend a lot of money. They'll hit a club with a few bucks in their pockets, spending it on the cheapest beer available and expecting a whole lot for very little from the dancers. The manager and staff at Dorsey's, established about thirty years ago and still going strong, aren't interested in pocket change. They want a clientele made up of businessmen, recently-divorced men looking to spend away their frustrations, and basically any guy over thirty, hopefully replete with credit cards.

A little after four I pulled up and parallel parked in front of the club. The parking lot angled behind the building only held about a dozen cars, so I easily could have parked in there.

But it was a gravel lot, surrounded on three sides by chain

link fence, and I figured it safer to be able to head out of there in a hurry if things went to hell.

Although I didn't intend for anything to go down, you never know.

I also assumed that the handful of cars in the lot, seeing as how they were all parked in the very back, belonged to employees rather than customers, and as I stepped inside it turned out I was right.

Dorsey's technically opens at three, but most nights the place doesn't start really hopping till around eight or nine, maybe a bit earlier on weekends. The first few hours they're open is actually the prep time for the bartenders, waitresses and dancers.

Actually, even using the term "bartender" is a bit of a stretch. Most nights they have one guy, maybe two, in a partioned area in back pouring out beer into plastic glasses, a bottle or two of whiskey and vodka on hand for the really high rollers.

Not exactly a place where the cocktail menu forms the main pull for customers.

When I stepped inside and managed to get my eyes adjusted to the dim lighting, I made out a grand total of one customer, a guy about my age sitting by himself at a table right in front of the stage. A skinny blonde wearing the bottom half of a black bikini gyrated on stage, her eyes vacant and stringy hair flopping every which way.

The customer wasn't even looking at her, instead focusing on the mug in front of him, and the lack of bills on the table in front of him indicated not much reward for the girl.

Aw, showbiz.

As I stood in the doorway, soaking in the ambiance, a young, thuggish-looking guy with a blond ponytail, like my hair going a bit gray, came my way.

"Sir?" he said, giving me the once over. "Can I help you?"

Ponytail Boy stood an inch or so over six feet and wore a white tee-shirt a size too small, probably in an attempt to make his impressive muscles look even larger. And although he looked big and imposing enough to cow drunken partiers with a single glance, he had the kind of gym- only physique that indicated he'd probably fall apart in a real confrontation.

"Tony," I said, "I'd like to see Tony."

"Mr. Adams is kind of busy. Is he expecting you?"

With my eyes, I did a 360 of the club. Still only the one dancer, looking damned near catatonic by this point, and her moribund customer.

The joint sure was hopping.

"Yeah," I said, "looks like he'd be busy as hell right now. Look kid, just tell Tony that Sam Quinton is here to see him, okay?"

I gave him the deadpan stare, which I'd perfected during my own brief tenure of bouncing clubs after I got hurt and before Duke Prowder took me under his wing.

The kid gave me a long, searching stare that kind of folded about halfway through, then nodded his head.

"Wait right here," he said before heading to the back part of the building. I stood there all of two minutes before Ponytail came out again, this time accompanied by Tony Adams.

"Bomber!" Adams called out from halfway across the room. The dancer and customer both looked our way for a second, then returned to their set poses. "How they hanging, guy?"

Tony Adams was one of those guys who could have been thirty or fifty, you just couldn't tell by looking at him. He'd been around the block for as long as I could remember, bouncing back and forth between KC and St. Louis, with every now and then a layover in Providence. He'd worked in various clubs and establishments, usually not the most reputable of places, and for the last three years, give or take, he'd been the manager of Dorsey's. The fact that he'd lasted so long in a place notorious for its turnover said something about him.

Like he was good at looking the other way.

"How you doing, Tony. Been a while, huh?"

"Too long, my man. Too long. So, what can I do for you? Ready to start bouncing my club?"

As he said that, Ponytail Boy looked kind of offended. Tony had offered me a job bouncing at least once a year since he'd taken over, no doubt thinking he could cash in somehow on my celebrity, or what remained.

"Sorry, Tony. I keep telling you, those days are behind me."

Now Ponytail scowled, as if I'd somehow demeaned his profession.

"Hey," Tony said. By this time, he'd gotten face to face with me and reached out to shake my hand. "Can't blame a guy. So, what can I do for you?"

I looked around the room in a slow, deliberate manner.

"Can we talk somewhere, Tony?"

"Sure, Blondie. Come on back."

A few seconds later we ended up in Tony's office, in the very rear portion of the building. A short hallway led from the main club room to his office, and as we traversed the hallway I noticed one of the rooms labeled "Dressing Room." From behind the closed door, I could hear the soft murmur of voices.

"You going to stay for part of the show?" Tony asked once we were seated in his office, each with a beer in our hand.

"Don't think I can, Tony. And this isn't exactly a social call."

While he furrowed his brow in puzzlement, I reached into my jacket pocket and pulled out a picture of Tammy Dodger, his deceased dancer.

As he glanced at the picture I could see the good humor drain out of his face.

"Oh, shit."

"Pretty much," I said. "It's a big pile of it, Tony. And it's just getting bigger."

"I heard that LeBow came to you."

"He did. After he found this girl of yours dead. And within twenty-four hours he was in the same state."

"But if he's dead, what does it matter to . . ."

"Let's call it an unpaid debt. Something that I owe him. What can you tell me about her?"

"What's to tell?" Tony shrugged his shoulders, presenting a picture of total innocence. "She worked here, sure. But that doesn't mean I knew anything about her. You know how it is. They come, they work a while, usually to make enough to buy their boyfriends' drugs, then they head on down the road. Doesn't really pay in the long run to get to know them too well."

Tony shook his head, a simple businessman perplexed by the oddities of the world.

"Tony," I said, "why don't you drop the bullshit? You and I both know that no one as smart as Paddy is going to let anyone, and I mean anyone, near any of his places without them being triple checked first. Somewhere, you've got a file on this girl that includes, among other things, her phone number, address and who to call in case of emergency. Considering the line of work, that's probably a friend or roommate. You probably even have all of her medical information. So why don't you get that file, the file you probably told the cops when they came around didn't exist, for me and let me go on my way. Or else."

For the first time, Tony looked as if he was taking me seriously.

"Or else what, Blondie?"

"Or else I'll probably take my frustration out on Ponytail out there, and you'll be looking for a new bouncer."

We locked gazes for about half a minute or so, Tony shifting back and forth on his feet. Finally, with his eyes crossed and perspiration forming on his forehead, I played one more card.

"Far as that goes, when all is said and done I'm going to guess that Paddy will be glad you gave it to me."

He reached for that straw quicker than the proverbial drowning man.

"You really think so?" he asked.

I nodded. I figured it at a fifty/fifty shot that Paddy would want me backtracking the girl, but I did my best to look a hundred percent assured.

Tony sighed and his shoulders went from a shrug to a slump.

"Okay," he said, "it's not like you can go around bothering her, right?"

He gave me a sickly smile and sat down behind his desk. Bending to the right, he rummaged around in a lower desk drawer for a minute, then brought up a single sheet of yellow paper. Handing it to me, I saw that it was an employment application for Tammy Dodger.

I frowned.

"How long did she work for you?"

"From the day she filled out the app. I hired her right on the spot." I glanced at the application date.

"Nearly nine months," I said.

Tony nodded.

"And you just happened to have her paperwork right on top of the drawer, like that?"

Tony grinned, though it didn't extend past his lips.

"Whatsa matter, Blondie? You get slapped around too much back in the ring? Of course not. I had her paperwork in the cabinet over there." He waved towards a dingy green, third-hand filing cabinet slumped in the corner. "Or at least I did, until a couple of cops came around the other day asking about her."

I shook my head at my own denseness.

"Soon as I heard about her on the news," he continued, "I pulled her stuff. Then it was only a matter of yes, officer, how else may I assist you officer, until they got the hell out of here and let me get back to business."

"And you just never got around to refiling her paper?" I asked.

Tony shrugged.

"I'm kind of surprised I didn't just toss it right away. What use do I have for it now?"

I glanced over the form and made a note of her address. She hadn't put down a phone number, and I knew the odds of the address being current, or even true, were slim, but I figured it wouldn't hurt to nail it down.

"You need anything else, Blondie?"

"Yeah," I said, "a couple more questions. When's the last time Paddy dropped by?"

A strange look came into Tony's eyes. Not just the typical

wariness of talking about the boss. A deeper, more feral fear seemed to ooze out of the guy.

"Paddy?" His voice rose about half an octave. "He drops by all the time. Sometimes to check the money, and sometimes just to check out the girls. You know?"

"How often?" I asked, and that odd fear lurking behind his gaze grew more pronounced.

"I told you, man. He comes in all the time."

"When's the last time you saw him?" I pressed.

"Just the other day."

I so wanted to invite Tony to play poker sometime, guessing I could clean up. But I also figured he'd gotten as specific as he would with me concerning his boss's comings and goings.

"One more thing," I said, "have you noticed any new guys around him lately? You know, not the old country crew he usually runs with?"

Tony's expression changed again. His jowls tensed and his nostrils flared.

"Yeah," he said, "I've met those guys. Bunch of pussies, you ask me. Not like the hard old guys Paddy usually uses."

Maybe so, but underneath the surliness I detected more of that fear Tony had been emanating since we'd entered his office.

"Okay, Tony," I said, "take care and thanks for the info."

"Anytime, Blondie. And hey, if you ever want it that bouncer job's always open." He grinned, weak and sickly.

"I'll keep it in mind," I said as I turned to leave the office.

CHAPTER EIGHTEEN

The complex was called Manor Gateway, though I didn't see any actual gate, and it sure didn't look like much of a manor. As soon as I'd seen the address on the form in Tony's office I'd figured what the place would look like, and I wasn't too far off.

It was one of five or six complexes, designed mainly for students, that had popped up in the last few years, circling around the university campus like a pack of slavering dogs. There'd been a time when our university had practiced the novel concept of capping the number of new students it admitted each year, a necessity in terms of controlling growth, ensuring classes didn't get overcrowded, and maintaining quality control of facilities.

About three or four years back, the powers that be decided to hell with such a rational approach and began amping up the number of students accepted. And as the numbers grew, in proportional terms, the quality went down, to the effect that we were now having a mini population explosion in our little town, most of it not to the good.

Among other things, seems like none of the city leaders and Ph.D's who'd instituted the new policy had considered that more young people, with some degree of disposable income, would serve as a magnet for some of the seedier levels of society.

Sure enough, along with higher population came more shootings, more drugs and more overall decline of life. Not that there was a direct cause and effect going on there, but the circumstantial evidence was kind of hard to overlook.

Then, just as the regular populace was standing around scratching its collective heads and wondering what the hell to do, the school made a couple of boneheaded public relations moves, and before you could blink the student numbers started plummeting like a cannonball thrown out of an airplane.

So much for level-headed civic planning.

Pulling into the common parking area of Manor Gateway, I saw about half the parking slots filled up. This close to the school, the majority of tenants would be students, but with evening coming on I assumed several would be home. The more people around, the more chances someone would be able to help me in my quest. That is, assuming my primary target wasn't home.

I parked in front of building A and looked over the complex.

Manor Gateway consisted of seven buildings forming a rough circle, with the parking area in the middle. A strip of asphalt peeking around the back corner of building A hinted at another parking lot behind, but looking as hard as I could, I couldn't spot the entry for it. All seven buildings went up three floors, and the balconies along the second and third floors sported an array of potted plants, exercise equipment and decorate thingies hanging down from overhead hooks.

The cars within sight, while not exactly luxurious, didn't seem to have a whole lot of body damage or cracked windows, and I only spotted a few oil stains here and there. Not luxury, for sure, but I'd seen places in town that looked a lot worse.

I got out of the Cherokee and headed towards the breezeway that sliced through building A. It only took a few seconds to figure the numbering system, and in no time, I stood outside the door of Apartment 10, the address for Tammy Dodger that I'd gotten off of her employment application.

Now came the uncertain part. I realized that the odds of the apartment still being in her name, after some months, were rather slim. Young ladies in her line of work tended to move around quite a bit, usually one step ahead of creditors or sleazebag ex-boyfriends. And I was pretty sure that Nichols and his folks had already checked out the address. Still, it would be sloppy to not at least give it a shot.

Not expecting much of anything, I knocked on the door of Apartment A10. Within a few seconds, it opened up.

"Yeah," said the young woman standing there. Brunette, around five four or thereabouts and probably no more than twenty-three, though with the amount of makeup, plus a general hardening of the lines in her face, I wouldn't have put money on it. Her body, attired in blue jeans and a pink tank top with the word "PURR" emblazoned across the chest, looked young, firm and, in one or two places, definitely enhanced, the letters on her tank stretched out about as far as they could get while the rest of her body was stick thin.

"Good evening," I said as I gave her the "aw shucks" grin. She gave me a blank look in return.

Maybe she mistook me for somebody's grandfather.

"What do you want?" she asked, a distinct huskiness in her tone. For a moment I thought of Kathleen Turner in *Body Heat*, though missing most of the class.

"My name's Sam Quinton," I said as I held out the little foldaway section of my wallet that held my license.

She looked closely at the license. Hard as I stared I couldn't see her lips move.

She may be able to help me after all.

"No shit? A private detective?" she said, giving me a distinct once over. "You don't quite look the part."

I shrugged.

"I get that a lot," I said.

She shook her head and turned back into her apartment. Not exactly an invitation, but I decided to take it as one.

"You can tell them they wasted their time sending you," she said as she moved over to a ratty cloth couch, which had two suitcases perched on it.

There was a certain stiffness to her movements, as if her

torso couldn't quite turn and bend as it should, and that husky voice had a bit of a quaver in it now.

"Oh yeah?" I asked.

"Yeah."

Besides the suitcases, a pile of women's clothes and toiletries were piled on the cushions, and she proceeded to jam various items into one of the pieces of luggage.

"Yeah," she repeated. "I got the message loud and clear." She turned and glanced at me over her shoulder. "As you can see, I'm heading out."

I nodded, scrambling my brain for a way to keep her talking without letting on that I didn't know what the hell she meant.

She finished stuffing the one case, but when she went to shut and clasp it she couldn't get the two sections all the way together. She struggled for a couple of seconds with no success and had turned around to sit on the case lid, when I walked over.

"Let me."

Frowning, she stepped out of the way, again not quite standing straight up.

She had way too much crap jammed in there, but in a minute or so I managed to get the lid shut and clasped.

"Thanks," she said.

I stared at her for a minute, then shook my head. "The hell with this. I'm guessing you're Tammy's roommate."

The young woman frowned. "You don't know? What kind of hood are you?"

"I'm not. I actually am a PI. It's not just a cover that allows me to carry a gun."

She took a step back, stumbling a bit, and held her hand up to her chest, doing her best to imitate a moll in an old film noir.

"But I thought. I mean, I assumed . . ."

"Why don't you raise your shirt up," I said. That still-pretty face hardened even more.

"Why do you . . ."

"'Cause I want to see just how bad they messed you up.

Don't worry. I'm not going to make a move. But I recognize the way you're moving. Hell, on more days than I would want to count I woke up moving the same way. Let's see just how bad it is. Lift your shirt. Not all the way off, just high enough."

She stood there, her face scrunched up with indecision. Then, after a couple of heartbeats, she grasped the bottom edge of her tee-shirt and began to lift it up. An inch high, then a couple of more, and about the time she exposed the bottom edges of her rib cage I saw pretty much what I'd expected.

A band of bruises formed the middle section of her torso. Dark purple mainly, with some crimson and a few streaks of green, probably took someone half an hour of wailing away on her to get that effect.

Whoever it was must have used their fists because if they'd used knucks or something similar instead of hobbling around her apartment she'd be on the floor with cracked ribs.

"You been to a doctor?" I asked, my own voice now kind of husky.

"What do you think?" she said. "Soon as I'm packed I'm getting out of here. Cops came around the other day and questioned me about Tammy. Told me not to leave town. Then a couple of hours later a few other guys show up and impress on me that I should leave. Who you think I'm going to listen to?"

"Why don't you sit down for a minute?" I said, gesturing towards an old, patched-up green recliner that sat in a corner of the room.

"I'm okay. I just need to . . ."

"You just need to take a minute and sit down. You may not be aware of it, since you're running basically on fear right now, but you're about out on your feet. Trust me, I've been hurt like that before and it damned near laid me out. And I'm a lot bigger than you are."

Something drooped behind those hard eyes, and she slumped a bit and flopped into the chair.

"Now," I stood close to her but not so close as to seem invasive, "what's your name?"

She sighed, as if the whole thing, strange men coming around, a brutal beating, and now another stranger, was just boring her.

"My name's Carol. Carol Lee. And yes, I'm—I was—Tammy's roommate."

"Could I take a leap and assume you also work at Dorsey's?"

The young woman nodded and dropped a bit lower in her chair.

"So, the cops came and questioned you about Tammy's death, right?"

"Right, mister. When she didn't come home Friday I didn't think much about it. After all, a girl's got to do her thing, right? But when I got to work Saturday she wasn't there, although we were supposed to have the same shift. I figured she must have gone off on some sort of lark. She did that now and then. By Monday I still hadn't seen or heard from her, and when I got to the club Monday night Tony told me what had happened."

"You two know each other long?" I asked.

"Long enough, I guess. We started working at Dorsey's about the same time, though we'd bumped into each other once or twice before. You know, around."

I nodded, my imagination easily filling in the gaps.

"Then, a few months ago Cici, the girl who used to live here, moved out."

"How come?"

Carol shrugged.

"Why else? She met a guy. One who was going to marry her and take her away from it all. Same old story."

"Did he? Marry her and take her away?"

Carol snorted, and those eyes hardened even more.

"What do you think? That jerk was with her long enough to snort up most of her cash. Last I heard, she was working hotel rooms. Giving hand jobs to college kids."

"Okay," I said.

"So anyway, I needed someone else to split the rent with,

and Tammy was looking for a place and . ." She lifted her hands, palms upwards.

"Got it," I said. "Let's get up to right now. The cops came around to question you, right? Probably a guy named Nichols?"

Carol nodded, though in kind of a subdued way. I couldn't see any marks there but wondered if they'd messed with her neck as well.

"Yeah, and they searched the place for about a day or so. I just got back and was putting things right again when these other dudes barged in."

"What'd they look like?" I asked, though I felt I already knew the answer. She snorted, but cut it off halfway and clutched her abdomen.

"God, that hurts like fuck. There were three of them, and they looked like accountants instead of hoods. I mean the whole jacket and tie thing."

"And you let them in?"

"Hell no." Now she glowered, though whether at me or the memory of the attack I wasn't sure. "I'm no goddamned fool. I looked through the peephole and thought at first they were selling something, but even if I had money I still would have told them to go away, which I did."

"Then how . . ."

I turned to look back at the door. I hadn't noticed any damage to it when I first showed up and still didn't see any.

"They knocked again. So, I went back and shouted to them through the door to leave me the fuck alone. At which point one of them said that if I knew what was good for me I'd look through the peephole again."

She stopped for a second, staring at me, but I stayed quiet.

"I figured just looking couldn't hurt," she continued, "but when I did I saw that one of those guys was holding some sort of handgun up to the door. You may have noticed this door isn't too thick, and he said if I did anything other than open up he would fire right through it."

"You let them in?"

Carol shrugged.

"I don't know all that much about guns, so I figured I couldn't take the chance."

"And when they came in . . ."

She gestured towards her stomach, which she had by now covered up.

"You saw."

I sat down on the end of the couch, next to one of the suitcases.

"What did they want?"

"Nothing much. Just wanted me to keep quiet and get the hell out of town. Which I'm doing."

She made a motion to her suitcases, then grimaced and clutched at her ribs. I stood up and went to support her.

"I'm okay," she half snarled as she tried to push me away. I was a lot bigger, and a lot more used to being pushed, and I didn't budge.

"No, you're not," I said. "You need a doctor. Probably should have had one a day or so ago."

"No!" she hissed, then swayed and leaned on my arm. Her face had paled even more, and I was afraid at any moment she'd begin spitting up blood. "They told me to leave. Said if I didn't they'd . . ."

"And you can leave. But not until you're able to move on your own. Come on."

I grabbed a denim jacket draped over a chair and shrugged her into it. Then I took her by the arm again and we headed out the door.

"Where are we going?" she asked.

I didn't really feel good about what I planned to do. I felt for the kid, sure, but I knew full well that I was about to use her to, hopefully, pop things wide open.

In other words, I was going to use her. Really not all that

different than all the sleaze balls, drowning in their beer, who groped and ogled her when she danced on stage.

But it had to be done. I needed a handle on this thing, and it looked like young, hard-bitten Carol Lee could turn out to be just the handle I needed.

CHAPTER NINETEEN

This time, there were two of us who didn't look like we belonged in the hotel, though I acknowledged the possibility of Carol being a bit more familiar with the place than me.

Different clerk this time, but we didn't entirely escape his glare as we passed through the lobby and toward the elevators.

I'd made a quick call to Nichols on the way over, just long enough to find out that they still had the Richards's home classified as a crime scene, and since I hadn't heard any different from the lady herself, I assumed the doc and his wife were still at the hotel.

The elevator doors opened up onto the Richards's floor.

As I stepped out, Carol held back, pinning me with a haunted, fearful gaze.

"What are you doing to me?" she asked.

"I'm getting you taken care of."

"Bullshit, mister. If that's what you had in mind, why not just take me to an emergency room? They'd treat me fine. Unless you're too cheap to spring for the bill?"

I shook my head, suddenly wondering if I had the fortitude to go through with my plan.

"Maybe the ER would be better," I said, "but they'd also have to report your injuries to the police, and I'm guessing you really don't want that."

She shuddered.

"God, no. All I want to do is get the hell out of this town."

"Let's get you checked out, and you can go."

But not, I didn't bother to tell her, until I'd gotten as much information as I could out of her.

* * *

Lucy Richards opened the door, an expectant look on her face. But when she saw my companion she took on the expression of an adult trying Sour Patch candies for the first time.

"Mr. Quinton?" she queried.

"Mrs. Richards, sorry to bother you. But my friend and I need to see your husband."

"After your last visit, he really doesn't want to talk to you. In fact, it would probably be best if we just . . ."

"Too bad," I said as I shouldered past her as gently as I could. I had Carol's wrist in my hand and guided her along with me into the suite.

The good doctor was reclining, appearing half asleep, on a couch up against the far wall, but when we entered he opened his eyes and stood up.

"You again?" he tried to pull off a thundering boom, but it came out as more of a squeak.

"Me again," I said, "companion in tow."

"I don't want you . . ."

"Right about now, doc," I put my best old-time Bomber sneer in my tone, "I don't really give a good goddamn what you want. I've got a friend here who's been hurt, hurt bad, and she needs medical treatment."

Carol stood by my side, her arm limp in my grip, looking around the suite.

Richards asked. "If she's hurt take her to a hospital. Why come by here?"

"Because it's best for her if no one knows she's still in town. And because I've got a hunch you know the people who hurt her."

Richards flinched at that. From the corner of my eye, I saw his wife's confused frown.

Richards himself tried to deflect.

"I'm retired. Besides, I was just a podiatrist. I couldn't possibly . . ."

"You're still a doctor. And you didn't study feet till the last year or so of med school. You've got an injured patient here, doc. Are you going to help or not?"

"Bill . . ." Mrs. Richards began.

"She doesn't look all that hurt to me," the old man said

For answer, I reached out and lifted Carol's tee-shirt up to just below her breasts. In the expensive, gleaming surroundings of the hotel suite her bruises shone in a ghastly hue.

Off to the side, Lucy Richards gasped.

"Still think she's okay," I disparaged. "And like I said, doc, I'm starting to think that you have a pretty good idea exactly who did this to her. What say you begin paying back your sins, huh?"

Lucy stifled a sob as she ran from the living room into one of the back rooms.

The wife may usually be the last to know, but this one was starting to get the idea that her husband had somehow messed up in a bad way.

Richards shrunk in on himself with his shoulders bowed and his head drooping. "I suppose you want the whole story," he said.

"Later. Right now, this young lady needs help."

Nodding, Richards walked across the room and took her by the hand. I figured they'd want some privacy, so I headed off into the rear portion to track down the missus.

With only one door back there shut, even someone with my limited detective skills could track her. I knocked on the door.

"Mrs. Richards? You okay?"

From the front part of the suite, I could hear the doc and his new patient mumbling.

The door opened, and Lucy Richards confronted me. She'd managed to get herself a little bit together.

"Kind of foolish, huh?" she asked.

"Not at all," I said as she opened the door to the bathroom and ushered me in.

"Bathroom" was not exactly the best description. The room was larger than my office back at the gym, probably even larger than the living room in my apartment. I walked over and took a seat on the rim of the tub.

The lady, not one easily embarrassed, plunked herself down on the toilet seat.

"So, am I fired?" I asked.

She looked up, brows puckering together.

"Why would you think that, Mr. Quinton?"

"Well, I'm guessing that this isn't exactly turning out as you'd hoped."

"Actually, I'm still trying to process it all. Would you mind giving me your appraisal?"

Sighing, I rubbed my palms over my thighs, purely as a way to give myself some time.

"Best guess," I finally said, "is that at some point in the past your husband got himself involved with some fairly bad people."

She nodded, her face still composed.

"His practice was always a success," she said, "enough so that we could live well. But for years I've had the suspicion that we were living a bit too much beyond our means."

"Like a month in France?"

She nodded again, at the moment not even looking at me. Instead, she seemed to be staring off into space, searching for some sort of big truth on the plain wall behind me.

"Yes, we've lived a fairly luxurious life, even by doctor standards."

"Most people think a medical degree is a license to print money."

She turned her gaze back to me. I saw resignation in those eyes, as if all the walls were starting to buckle, but I also saw something else.

"Most people don't know what the hell they're talking

about," she said. "Yes, doctors can make decent money, as long as they live in a fairly well-populated area. But by the time you deduct daily expenses, plus malpractice insurance, unemployment contributions and student loans, you're suddenly not talking as much disposable income as some would think. And for sure not enough to enjoy the lifestyle we've lived for years."

"You pretty much figured that the good doctor had some other source of income?"

She nodded, and reddened a bit around the eyes.

"I'm an old-fashioned woman, Mr. Quinton. I stopped working six months after Bill and I got married. Spent the next thirty plus years raising our children and taking care of the home. I paid most of the household bills, and it's not like I'm an ignoramus when it comes to money, but I also didn't question too closely his exact income. Just took it for granted that we were living charmed lives."

"Until you had to cut your vacation short because of a murdered woman in your house," I said.

She twisted her hands together.

"What exactly is he involved in?" she asked. "Do you know yet?"

A short cry came from the front portion of the suite. I hoped it was just a matter of the elderly doctor being a little rough with his examination.

"I don't know for sure yet," I said, "but my guess is that your husband was supplementing his income by being a mob doctor."

"A what?"

I felt like hell as I considered the amount of damage I was about to do to their marriage, but that was just emotion. If anyone had harmed their lives, it was Richards himself.

"A doctor on call, if you will. I think at some point in the past he hooked up with the local faction of organized crime and came to an arrangement. For a steady infusion of cash, he'd be available to patch up any injuries that they didn't want to go to a hospital for."

It was a good thing the lady was sitting down, or I could imagine her falling to the floor.

"You mean he works for the Mafia? Like on a retainer? Do we even have such a thing here in Providence?"

Another slight mewling sound came from the outer room. I suspected the thugs who'd visited Carol had broken a rib or two.

I shrugged in answer to her question.

"As far as Mafia, I'm guessing we may have one or two trace elements. After all, with KC and St. Louis on either side of the state, it's hard to imagine that some of the boys don't occasionally visit. But no, that's not quite who I mean."

"Then who?"

That red puffiness had left her eyes now, and a new shade of red, an angry crimson, was flushing her face.

"This is just a guess, so far, Mrs. Richards, though I think it's a pretty educated guess. I think your husband is hooked in with a guy named Paddy O'Brien."

"Sounds Irish."

"He is most definitely Irish. And he's also one of the roughest, most ruthless independent gangsters in the state. He has his own crew. As far as I know he's beholden to no one, though he must have some sort of arrangement with the larger syndicates. But when it comes to organized crime here in Providence and within about a hundred-mile radius, Paddy is the man."

"And you think my husband is employed by him? To do what? Patch up his goons when they get hurt?"

"I do, plus anyone affiliated who may get injured along the way."

"But that doesn't make any sense." Smart woman here, and she wasn't taking anything I said at face value. "If Bill works for this O'Brien person, then why would they have murdered that girl in our home?"

I had a hunch about that, but I wasn't about to speculate until I had something a bit more solid.

Fortunately, just then someone knocked on the door.

"You can come out now," Dr. Richards said from the other side of the panel.

When his wife and I stepped out into the suite at large, I saw Carol sitting on the couch, slightly hunched over, her face contorted.

"How is she?" I asked.

"Could have been worse. She'll be in a lot of pain for a month or so. I think there's some hairline fractures on a couple of her ribs, but when I suggested she get an X-ray she shut me down."

That made sense, considering Carol's earlier insistence on just getting out of town.

"I gave her a prescription for some pain medicine. Not as good as she could get at a hospital, but better than nothing."

I must have looked my question because the older man set himself in a defensive posture.

"You may have guessed, Mr. Quinton, that I'm not exactly as retired as I pretend to be. I still carry around a prescription pad. You'd be amazed how often it comes in handy."

From the corner of my eye, I saw his wife wince.

"I don't doubt it," I said. "But that leaves one other little thing."

This whole time Carol had sat on the couch, not even looking our way, and I began to wonder just what the doc had doped her with.

"Which would be what?" Richards asked.

"She needs to disappear. That's what the whole beating was about, to convince her to leave. And I want to help her do just that."

"What's your point?" Richards asked.

"My point is she needs some money. She's got maybe a couple of hundred on her, which will get her just a county or two over, and one night in a motel will eat most of it up."

"Mr. Quinton, I hope you're not implying what . . ."

"I'm not implying it, doc. I'm saying it flat out. How much do you have on you?"

Richards drew himself up to his full height, no doubt as an attempted power play. But since I towered a good six inches over him regardless, it didn't have a whole lot of effect.

"I've had just about enough of you, mister," Richards worked to get outrage in his tone, but it came out as a shaky squeak.

"I don't care what you've had," I said, walking a few steps into his space and putting on my most threatening look from back in my ring days. "That girl's in trouble because of something you've had a hand in. I don't know yet what, but I'm sure as hell going to find out. Whatever it is, it's gotten at least two people killed, and I have a feeling a friend of mine is in serious trouble. Grab your wallet and checkbook and let's see just what you've got."

He tried to straighten himself even more, and for a moment I wondered if I was going to have to actually get physical with him.

"Bill," Lucy Richards said from off to the side, "get him the goddamned money."

It was the first time I'd heard her come even close to cursing, and it made me like her a whole lot more.

CHAPTER TWENTY

I dropped Carol off at the bus station. We'd managed to leave the hotel suite with nearly two grand in her pocket. Not enough to get very far, but at least she could make it out of the state. On the drive over, she'd said something about a cousin who lived in Minnesota, and I'd told her to make sure they were absolutely trustworthy before showing up there.

My best guess was that the guys who'd threatened her would be satisfied with her splitting town. If they'd wanted more than that, they would have done some real damage. If they'd really wanted to make a statement, they would have scarred either her face or her body, making it tough for her to get work again.

Once the bus pulled away, I figured she was fairly safe, at least from your standard run-of-the-mill mobster.

The problem was, I wasn't all that sure that who we were dealing with counted as run-of-the-mill.

And as a side note, I realized I had just possibly, in a major way, interfered with an ongoing police investigation. It was the kind of thing that could easily cost me my license and would have had old Duke kicking my ass all across town.

As I climbed into my Cherokee, I keyed my cell phone and gave Nichols a call.

"What's up?" he said as soon as he picked up.

"Wondered if you'd be interested in having dinner with a civilian," I said.

"The civilian being you?"

"My treat," I said.

"Oh, really. What'd you do now?"

"Josh, we're friends. All I'm doing is inviting you to dinner."

"Of course, that's all. Right when I'm in the middle of two cases, both of which involve you and both of which the lieutenant told you to stay out of. Yet you're still dogging around them, aren't you?"

I flicked my signal and eased out of the parking lot and onto the street. As I did so, I saw a cherry-red Nova, complete with yellow flames up and down the sides, pull out behind me.

Seriously?

"I don't know what you mean by dogging around," I said.

"Maybe I mean that you've been spotted going in and out of the hotel where our displaced homeowners are staying. What about that?"

I hung a right and headed towards the city's western outskirts. The Nova turned with me, though going slow enough that it hung back nearly a block. Checking to make sure I wouldn't irritate anyone unnecessarily, I slowed down to about five under the speed limit.

"Me visiting them is legitimate," I told Nichols, "at least partly. Mrs. Richards hired me to make sure that they weren't in any danger."

It was a partial truth, at best, but Nichols wasn't buying it.

"Did you happen to mention, as she was dangling a check in front of you, that that's what they pay police for?"

I glanced in the mirror. Cherry red was still hanging back there.

"What can I say? They got called home from vacation unexpectedly because of a dead stripper in their house. Maybe she thought something like that needed personal attention."

"To protect them? Or to find out if her husband had any involvement in the mess?"

I stopped at a red light, the Nova pulled up three car lengths back. Squinting, I did my best to get a look at the occupants, but the smoked-over windows defeated me.

"Actually," I said, "a little of both. Don't take it personal, but the whole thing spooked her, so I said I'd look into it."

"Uh huh," Nichols didn't sound a whole lot convinced. "And were you hired before or after your little jaunt out to Paddy's?"

The light turned green, and I gunned the Cherokee's engine. Whipping across lanes, I did a way illegal U-turn, causing half a dozen horns to start honking around me. Gunning back the way I'd just come, I looked up to see red Nova cutting across the lanes much as I had.

Okay, I thought. It's not some sort of soft tail.

My breath came faster, and the sweat on my palms made the steering wheel slick.

"What the hell was that?" Nichols asked in my ear.

"Josh," I said, "I'm on Culbert, heading east. If you've got any cars in the neighborhood, I'd suggest you get them over to the Westway parking lot right now."

The Nova was steadily creeping up on me. Only two car lengths behind, they obviously had given up on even trying to act discrete and were homing in on me as quick as they could.

Not bothering to signal, I cut to the right again and ended up in the parking lot of the strip mall I'd mentioned to Nichols. I strained my ears for the sound of sirens but didn't hear anything.

A split second later, the Nova came barreling up alongside

Edging into early evening of a weekday, there wasn't a whole lot of traffic, either vehicular or human, in the area, but there was still more than I wanted. I spotted the comparative emptiness of the north end, which housed an alteration shop and Christian book store, and gunned my vehicle that way.

It wasn't just my palms sweating now, and I was wondering just how badly I'd misjudged the situation.

Doing something that resembled a half bootlegger's turn, the Cherokee rocked to a stop, the driver's side facing the Nova. I scooted across the seat and tumbled out the passenger's door, collecting a moderate number of scrapes and burns from the asphalt as I landed.

For a slight moment, which felt like an hour, no movement or sound came from the Nova. A couple of bystanders had gathered at the other end of the strip, craning their heads in order to see the action. I assumed some of them would film it with their phones and wondered just how much publicity the has-been wrestler The Blond Bomber was about to get.

Publicity which wouldn't do me a whole lot of good if I was dead. And where the hell were the cops?

The protracted nanosecond snapped to an end, and the Nova's doors popped open.

I'd had a hunch all along that the occupants wouldn't be the blazer-wearing clones from the other day, and I was right.

Three tried and true gangbangers, Hispanic from the looks of them, rushed out of the Nova, automatic weapons out and ready.

Well, hell, I thought. Here we go.

CHAPTER TWENTY-ONE

Most people sneer at pro wrestling as fake, which in a way it is. But those of us in the biz, both current and former, prefer the word "scripted." In other words, when you enter a match you know more or less how it's going to go and who's going to come out the winner. But all those individual moves, flips and slams are kind of made up on the fly by the performers. And despite what most people think, not all of those punches and impacts are pulled or softened. Every now and then, performers can get carried away, lose their temper or just be flat out inexperienced. In which case, some of those slaps, punches and slams are real. And they hurt.

In the ring, it's easy to look like you're a tough guy, and when you walk into a bar or club and puff your chest out, you can usually carry that off without too much hassle. Sure, there's the occasional drunken moron who challenges you to a fist fight, but half the training is how to keep from getting hurt, while the other half is how to keep from injuring your opponent. So even with the wasted loud mouths, it's easy to handle things, giving you more and more the conviction that you really are one tough hombre.

Until the day when three gangers come out of a red Nova and begin spraying the immediate vicinity with their Glocks.

Or whatever guns they had. I just say Glocks because everyone and their mother seem to think that's the only brand of gun to carry. For damned sure, I wasn't taking the time to look too closely. At that point, even with my bouncing, security and investigative experience, I didn't find it quite so easy to remember how tough and indestructible I was.

I glanced to both sides. For at least fifty feet in either direction, I couldn't see anything that would constitute solid cover. The bangers were continuing to make a mess of the Cherokee, either from the deluded conviction that I was still inside or from sheer derangement.

I had my own weapon in hand, but against the three of them it seemed so inconsequential I didn't even want to fire. I only had nine bullets in the clip, and I don't need the weapon often enough to carry one under the hammer, so I wanted to use them as sparingly as possible.

Finally, I heard sirens. They sounded a long ways off, but the constant hammering of shells into the car body had numbed my ears so much that I couldn't reliably gauge distance.

Amazingly, not a single cartridge had yet come near me, scooched down as far into the pavement as I could get. Looking back on it later, I'd probably realize that all of that action had taken place within just a few seconds from when it began, so in another moment or two my assailants would either spot me or guess where I was, and that would be the end.

I set myself in a straight line backwards from the Cherokee and lumbered my pistol in front of me. If I had to go, I could at least take out an ankle or two before they got me.

I heard a louder, much more solid gunshot, almost like from a .44. From my angle of vision, I could only see the bottom half of legs, but suddenly one of the bangers, the one on my left, plumped to the asphalt, his head nearly split in two. I saw the sudden shifting of legs of the other two, angling towards the left.

What the hell?

Two more of those booming shots, and two more sets of legs, along with the bodies attached to them, went tumbling to the pavement. After that, a momentary silence, save for the rapidly-approaching sirens.

Now a third car, a newer Lincoln, came squealing to a stop alongside of me. As the Lincoln's window rolled down, two men came from around the strip mall's corner, holstering large automatics.

"Blondie," a voice called from inside the Lincoln, "you may want to speed it up a bit."

I felt like I was moving slowly, but realized later I must have been going fairly quickly, as I climbed to my feet and jogged the few yards to the Lincoln. The rear door nearest to me opened at the same time as the two strangers climbed into the passenger's side, and I crawled into the back driver's side and found myself face to face with Paddy O'Brien.

"Thanks," I said as the driver hit the gas and got us out of there, only a few seconds ahead of the cops.

As we merged into the normal traffic and assumed a more sedate speed, I glanced at the two gunmen who were now settled in their seats and staring out the windows.

I looked back at my savior. "What the hell, Paddy?"

CHAPTER TWENTY-TWO

"It's a war," Paddy said.

"No shit," was my brilliant, pithy response.

It had been ten minutes since we'd left the scene of the throwdown and since we'd pulled up in the driveway of a plain-looking white house on the western edge of town, right before the city gives way to the rolling hills of the country.

While this area was technically in the city limits, half an acre or so of woods surrounded each house, and most of the driveways slanted either up or downhill.

On the one hand, the kind of area it could be dangerous to be surrounded in, but with all those trees you could range a platoon of lookouts around your location, which I was guessing Paddy had done.

During the drive, we hadn't talked much at all. Me because I was trying to manfully cover up the shakes threatening to tear me limb from limb and Paddy, hell, I had no clue why Paddy hadn't said anything. Except that each time I glanced sideways at him, his face had become tighter and paler.

Though he would never show it, I sort of assumed he was almost as scared as I was.

Once we entered the house, Paddy left me in the living room and went back through a door into the kitchen. Without a word, his associates who had accompanied us split up, a couple going upstairs and the others, turning back outside.

Shrugging, I headed over to a recliner and made myself comfortable.

About thirty seconds later, Paddy came back into the room, a couple of Heineken bottles clutched in the fingers of his right hand. His left hand held a 9mm.

Handing me a bottle, he settled himself on a couch facing me and popped the cap on his. I did the same, and in unison we both took a long, deep swig.

"Ahh," Paddy said as he came up for air. "Boy, did I need that."

"So, what the hell's going on, Paddy?"

"It's a war."

"No shit."

* * *

Paddy settled back and took another long pull on his beer.

"I'm guessing you heard about Don Lipardo, right?"

The seeming non-sequitur threw me for a moment, and I had to struggle to get my thoughts on track. "Sure," I said, "but that was over half a year ago."

Don Anthony Lipardo had run the St. Louis Mafia family for several decades. Although he had a street reputation as a brutal, no-nonsense gangster, he'd gotten through most of his career with a relatively low profile, at least as far as the general public went. But for the last few years, strange rumblings had come out of the eastern part of the state, and to those who kept an eye on such things, it became obvious that Lipardo's control, whether through age or something else, had begun to slip.

And at the same time, the boys from Kansas City had started slipping into St. Louis county and, so the stories went, begun to take over parts of his operation.

About six months back Lipardo had dropped from sight and

no one, at least no one who was talking, seemed to have a clue as to where he'd gone. The prevailing theory, among those in the know, held that he'd been ambushed by the KC mob, his body lying somewhere deep and dark.

"As you probably know," Paddy said, "Don Lipardo and I had a good arrangement for a lot of years."

"Right. You gave him a stipend each year, and he left you alone and kept any other interested families out of the middle of the state. But it wasn't that much of a sacrifice for him."

Paddy stared at his almost-empty bottle for a minute.

"What you mean by that?"

"Let's face it, Paddy. Even with the area growth of the last several years, there's really not that much here that makes it worth anyone's while to mount a takeover."

For a second there, Paddy's eyes hooded over and his neck developed a slight flush, but then he nodded and finished off the rest of his drink.

"You always were a smart kid, Blondie. Did you ever run into any of Tony's boys when you performed around St. Lou?"

I shrugged.

"Every now and then. Socially, you know. Hanging out in bars after the shows. Way I figure it, those guys get enough of actual violence in real life that they don't have that much interest in the make-believe type. And it's not like there was enough money in the federation to act as any kind of a lure."

"Hah!"

He stood up and went back into the kitchen. Stopping in the doorway, he glanced my way and lifted his eyebrows, but I shook my head.

He came back in a moment later, another Heineken in his hand.

"I had things running pretty good with Lipardo. Then he went and pulled his vanishing act, and the KC family comes a calling."

I nodded.

"Word has it that Lipardo's no longer with us," I said.

Paddy shrugged. "Don't look at me, guy. Your guess's good as mine. All I know is that with him no longer reaching out and his territory pretty much up for grabs, no one in St. Lou has time to worry about an old, second-hand Mick operation like mine."

"No one in St. Louis," I stressed.

"Correct."

"Let me guess," I said. "KC wants to work off a different business model than you and the don used, right?"

"That's a nice way of putting it, Blondie."

"What's the not so nice way?"

"One day, a week or so after everyone stopped hearing from Don Lipardo, one of the KC caporegimes shows up. Actually drives into Longton and knocks on my front door. Says that it's time to renegotiate, that it's time for some quality control and efficiency in my operation."

"The clones," I said.

"The what?"

"All those spit-and-polish guys you've got hanging around. The ones who drove off your old crew. I'm guessing they don't belong to you, do they?"

Paddy stared into his bottle for a moment, but I doubt that he found what he was looking for there.

"Clones," he finally said. "Sounds like something Rogan would say. Well, guess that's as good a term as any. And you guessed right. They belong to the KC boss, setting up their new order of doing business."

"No more goombahs running around, huh?"

Paddy chuckled. "The goombah's, as you call them, basically went out with Gotti and the RICO act. But, yeah, you got the basic idea."

Something about all this just didn't sit right with me, almost as if the man sitting across from me spinning this story were a total stranger.

"It doesn't wash, Paddy."

"Meaning?"

"Meaning the Paddy O'Brien that I know would never just roll over for a threat like this. The guy I knew would fight like hell to keep what's his, and he for damned sure wouldn't ever bail out on men who'd been loyal to him for years. How about telling me the whole story?"

I noticed his hand, the one holding the bottle, tightening, and for a second, I worried he was going to shatter the glass. But his face tightened, his jaw squared, and very deliberately he put the beer down on the coffee table in front of him.

"Times change, Sam. That's all there is to it. I saw the writing on the wall and decided to go with the changes."

"So, what ruined it?"

"Huh?"

"Why the running gun battles? And what the heck does all this have to do with Dr. Richards, not to mention the two murder victims?"

Paddy went quiet again, back to searching for whatever he hoped to find reflected in that green bottle. I gave him the time, partly because I was interested in what he had to say and partly because I didn't have a clue what to do next.

"I've had enough," he mumbled, more to himself than to me.

"Say what?"

"I said I've had enough of it. When you've been on top as long as I have, you can only take so much of not being your own man anymore. And I reached that point."

Something lowered behind his eyes , and I knew he'd said all he had to say on the subject. But I hadn't heard nearly enough.

"I need more, Paddy."

"More what?"

"More of all of it. I need to know more about the KC boys, what they're having you do that you somehow can't stomach and what Dr. Richards, LeBow and Tammy Dodger had to do with any of it."

Paddy tilted his head back and finished his beer. I'd only drunk about three sips out of mine.

He brought his gaze level with me.

"Okay, Blondie. I guess it's time to tell the tale."

CHAPTER TWENTY-THREE

I had the car drop me off outside my gym a little after one the next morning. I'd barely shut the door before the driver sped off, but I in no way took it personal. After spending the last several hours holed up with Paddy, I didn't really care about how jumpy anyone else may have been.

Going in through the backdoor was maybe a little bit of an over precaution, but it was clear by now that the out of towners were well aware of my connection, however peripheral, to Paddy. Shortly after getting the debriefing from Paddy, I'd borrowed a burner phone to place a call, and the recipient of that call was waiting for me inside my office.

"Funny," I said as I tossed my jacket onto one of the empty chairs, "I don't remember giving you a key."

"Well, do me a favor and don't tell anyone I broke in," Josh Nichols said. "The way things have been for cops in general the last couple of years, I'd probably end up in Leavenworth."

I sat down behind my desk and reached into one of the drawers for a bottle of Maker's Mark. Raising the container in Nichols's direction, I canted my eyebrow at him.

"Why not," my cop buddy said. "I've been off duty for all of an hour or so."

"Crime rate in town dropping?" I asked as I poured generous portions into two glasses.

"You know better than that," Nichols said as he reached for his glass. "If anything, I'm betting you know a lot more than I do. Like what happened to a certain roommate of one of our recent murder victims. Someone we specifically wanted to keep in town just in case we needed her to build a case. Or just where O'Brien, who seems to have fallen off the radar, may be found. You know anything about any of that stuff?"

Leaning back, I took a long drink, allowing the liquor to slowly make its way through my system. It was the best I'd felt in a couple of days, which wasn't really saying a whole lot, and at the moment it wouldn't have taken much for me to just drift off and spend the rest of my life inside that bottle.

Except, of course, for the fact that I had things to do.

"I'm not sure I know more than you do, Josh, but I know a hell of a lot more than I did just twenty-four hours ago."

"Like what?"

"Like I've got a pretty good hunch who killed Tammy Dodger, though I'm still not sure why. Same with LeBow. And I know that you've got one hell of a problem breathing down your neck. Actually, all of us do."

Nichols took a fairly lengthy pull of his drink, then raised his gaze up to meet mine. "Sounds like you've been busy."

I shrugged.

"More like right place, right time, and doing a lot of listening. Amazing what you can hear when you keep your mouth shut."

"People tell me," Nichols said. "And I'm guessing all of this came from a particular Irish hoodlum that a lot of my colleagues have been wanting to lock up for years?"

I shrugged again before finishing off my drink. "What can I say, Josh. I run in unique social circles."

"Where is he?" Nichols's tone had suddenly dropped a few degrees of warmth.

"Where he'll be safe for now," I said. "Or at least as safe as he can be. Trust me, Josh. I'm serious when I say you've got bigger problems than slapping the cuffs on Paddy."

"He's at least peripherally involved in two murders in the last several days, in case you've forgotten."

"I haven't forgotten, Josh. What I'm trying to tell you . . ."

"Then tell me, then. Just what is so goddamned important that you . . ." "

A war," I said.

"Huh? What kind of—you mean a mob war?"

"That's exactly what I mean. You know all the crap that's been flying in St. Louis the last few months, ever since the old man disappeared?"

"Yeah."

"Well, some of the blowback's happening in our own fair town," I said. "Actually, I'm kind of surprised the feds haven't already descended on us like a plague."

Nichols squirmed in his seat, literally squirmed. Like a first-grader caught giggling at a dirty joke in class. "Maybe they have," he said.

I raised my empty glass to him, at the same time wondering just how out of the loop I was in my own town. "Looks like we're the grand prize winners," I said.

Nichols dug into his jacket pocket, pulled out his phone and hit one of the buttons.

"You calling the lieutenant?"

"What do you think?" he said.

"I think maybe you better wait until I give you the whole story."

My buddy froze, holding his phone by the side of his head. "Come again?"

"There's a lot that's been going down here, Josh. You'd better let me give it to you straight, or as straight as I can, before you call anyone. And maybe you can give me what you can on your side of it."

"You're assuming there's something different on my side?" he asked.

I nodded.

"Be hard to believe there wasn't."

Nichols lowered the phone, his eyes taking on a hooded look. Although he was my friend, he was a cop more than anything, and I could guess he didn't like my implication

"You think there's problems in the department?" he asked, his voice hitting a lower pitch.

Providence likes to think of itself as a big city, but it's actually a fairly small town. At least, in all the ways that matter. We've got over a hundred thousand citizens, with slightly less than half long-term residents, and a small fraction of that doing most of the real moving and shaking around town.

Our entire police department could fit in a small high-school gym. Same for the fire department, and the EMS crew could squeeze into a standard office.

In other words, fair-sized metro area or not, the folks that matter are few.

And very, very tight.

"You think we've got some dirt on the inside?" Nichols repeated.

"No," I said, though I did have reservations about one or two in the department.

However, despite our friendship, I couldn't imagine Nichols siding with me over his department, not unless he had rock solid proof.

I was keeping my suspicions in check, at least for a while.

"I'm just saying that everyone's going to have to move really careful or the fallout from this is going to be immeasurable."

I poured myself another slug, then held the bottle out to him again. When Nichols shook his head, I capped the bottle and put it away. I figured a second drink was all I could take at the moment, and even that might be pushing it.

"So, talk," my buddy the cop said.

* * *

"How much did you dig up about Richards?" I began.

"The doctor? He checks out clean, at least as far as we can tell. He's just what he looks like. A retired podiatrist."

"Right. A foot doctor. When you answered the call on the dead girl, what did you think of his house?"

Nichols shrugged. "I'd like to live there."

"Does it seem like the kind of place your average doctor could afford?"

Another shrug. "Doctors make a lot of bank, you know that."

"Josh," I grimaced, "please don't try to sound like a hip twenty-year old. And one doesn't make a lot of bank. That's redundant. You just make bank."

Nichols grinned and leaned back in his chair. "What are you getting at, buddy?"

"Simply that most doctors, even at their best, couldn't afford to live in a place like the Richards's do. They make a lot of money, most of them, especially if they specialize. But a good specialty is brain surgery or ophthalmology. Maybe pediatrics. But podiatry?"

Nichols gave me a blank look, which usually means his mind is spinning.

"Furthermore," I continued, remembering what Mrs. Richards had told me and wanting to show how smart I was, "even if they earn a lot of dough, by the time they've paid for malpractice insurance, office upkeep and help, various fees and licenses, not to mention the daily bills, they . . ."

"Okay, okay." Nichols waved me away. "You're saying there's something hinky about the doc? Something suspicious about the way he earned all that dough?"

"Close but not quite. I'm saying he never did earn all that much, at least not by rich people's standards. He just lived far, far beyond his means. And he had other problems."

"Gambling?"

I nodded, Nichols shook his head.

"Let me guess," he said, "that's how he got onto O'Brien's radar."

"Richards was running up debt, and Paddy's in a business where from time to time his associates need medical attention."

"You saying the kindly retired medic is actually a mob doctor?"

"Mob with a small 'm,'" I said. "We both know that Paddy's nothing but a mid-sized fish in a tiny pond."

"With no desires to become anything bigger."

"Right, or he would have done so long before now. So, the doctor fixed up Paddy's boys, on the few occasions they needed it, plus performed a variety of services for the girls at his club, and everything's copasetic."

"Until?" Josh asked, though clearly, he'd already gotten there.

"Until Paddy's protector in St. Louis pulls a disappearing act, and the western half of the state decides it's time to move in."

"We decided to put a guard on him yesterday. At the behest of you know who in Washington, but we were about to do the same anyway." Nichols gave me another of those searching gazes. "But he seems to have gone to ground somewhere. So far, we haven't been able to track him down."

I nodded, keeping my expression as non-committal as possible. The area wasn't all that large or complicated, and sooner or later the cops would track Paddy down. But without knowing more about the overall lay of the land, I didn't want to point any fingers too soon.

"He's in the wind?"

"Probably just as well. Sounds like these clowns have sat through too many viewings of *The Godfather*," Josh said.

"Maybe, but the way I hear it, St. Louis is mostly gone, except for a few hardcases wanting to make a final stand."

"And just who do you hear that from?"

I waved that one away, and Nichols sighed. "Enter Providence," he said.

I nodded.

"It's far enough away that they can move around relatively undetected, but close enough that in a few hours on the interstate they can be back in their old stomping grounds."

"Except," Josh prodded.

"Except that, again through the grapevine, KC factored

that in ahead of time, and they've already got their hooks into Paddy."

"I'm guessing O'Brien didn't take to the idea."

"You're guessing right. But with Lipardo only God knows where, probably dead, he didn't have much of a choice."

"Dead," Nichols said.

"Huh?"

"Don't repeat this to anyone, especially any stray Irishmen you happen to stumble over, but the common consensus is that Lipardo bought it back when. Now, they're just scouring the area trying to find the body."

"I'm not sure if that simplifies or complicates things, Josh. I'm assuming that Kronberg's running point on this?"

"As much point as he can. Clearly, this is a fed matter, and they've been quietly sending out feelers all over the state for a while now."

"KC is pretty much in charge of the city, Josh."

"Jesus Christ!" Nichols spit out. "No one's talking about it being that bad yet. All this has been going down without us even knowing it?"

"Don't feel too bad," I said. "These younger mob guys aren't the Gotti knockoffs most people imagine. Hell, one or two of them even know how to use e-mail."

"And all of this has exactly what to do with Richards, LeBow and the dead girl?"

"That's what I'm still working on. All I can tell you for sure is Paddy's running scared, but I haven't quite nailed why his off-the-books doc is so central to the whole thing. Hell, with as many medical professionals as we have in the area, why is one retired sawbones so damned important?"

"Christ," Josh repeated. "Could this get any more clustered?"

I stared at Nichols, wondering if the question were rhetorical or not.

"Do you really want to know?" I asked.

CHAPTER TWENTY-FOUR

The mob was the cops' problem, of course, but I had stuff to deal with on my own. As far as I knew, I was still employed, at least nominally, by Lucy Richards. So, after a few hours of sleep, a quick workout and a shower, I headed out.

I was five steps out the door before I realized I didn't have a vehicle. My Cherokee, I guessed, was still parked where I'd left it, full of bullet holes from the goons Paddy had saved me from. Actually, by now it had probably been towed off somewhere and was waiting for me in the county impound lot

Nichols hadn't mentioned it, but then we'd had bigger things to discuss.

I wheeled back into the gym. In my office I had a small, old-fashioned personal address book. I kept it around because there were some numbers I didn't want to end up in someone else's hands if something happened to my cell phone. It took only a minute or so to look up the number of an old buddy from my wrestling days and, after thirty seconds or so of grumbling at my calling him so early, plus another two minutes of his bragging about the blonde he'd met last night who now slumbered on the other side of his bed, he agreed to climb out of his warm bed and loan me his car.

Forty minutes later, I was tooling through the streets in a year-old dark maroon Mustang.

Downtown Providence stays rather quiet in the early

morning. We're not exactly the rowdiest of towns, but during the school year, when all the colleges are in session, there's usually some activity, even if of the quiet sort, around downtown. Things usually taper off for the young people around three or four, and the business folks and day workers don't start showing up till seven o'clock on. Driving through the deserted section, with the clock hovering around six, I kind of felt like the last man on earth. Instead of pulling into the parking garage, I decided instead to park in one of the numerous empty slots on the street outside the hotel.

It was a little too early to be calling on anyone, especially a retired couple in their late golden years, but I wanted a chance to catch the good doctor off guard, maybe shock him into some truth.

Turns out, I needn't have bothered.

If the front desk clerks had looked askance at me on my first few visits to the place, the early morning man gave me an absolutely venomous glare. I smiled as sweetly as possible and, tired as I was after the last few days of playing games, really didn't give a damn.

The elevator took me up to the penthouse level, and as the doors opened I had my game plan firmly in mind. I'd already shared my suspicions with Lucy Richards earlier, but now Paddy had all but confirmed things. I wanted to confront the doctor, in front of his wife, get him to confess as to exactly how, and with whom, he'd been supplementing his income for so long, then pressure him to find out exactly what it was the KC boys wanted. Whatever it was, it must be big for them to consider two murders as acceptable collateral damage.

When I took three steps out of the cage and turned the corner to my right, all my plans changed.

Mainly because I saw two goons outside of the Richards's door, one standing guard and the other using what looked like a passkey to get them inside.

A man in uniform lay face down on the floor, blood seeping from a head wound.

I puzzled over that one for a nanosecond, till I took a second look at the outfit he wore.

Dude was a private security guard, which told me that the doc and his wife weren't quite as clueless as they let on.

Later on, when I had time, I'd probably feel professionally slighted. If they wanted a bodyguard, I could have provided Lucy with several good names. Then again, hiring security could have been the doc's idea, and she couldn't have objected without letting on that she'd already hired me.

Unless she'd given up on me, considering my seeming lack of progress over the last few days.

All that sort of self-moping would have to wait for later. Right now, I had more immediate things to worry about.

The guy playing lookout noticed me at the same time I saw him, and from there it was pretty much a race to see who could overcome their surprise quickest and make the first move.

Turned out to be pretty much a draw.

The guard came my way while the other continued his work at the door. These two weren't clones, those faceless guys in their blazers and ties. The one facing me towered over me by at least four inches and would probably have ripped out of a size 46 jacket.

He wasn't one of Paddy's old-time guys, at least he didn't look very Irish, so I figured him for just cheap labor hired by the hour.

Even so, he knew how to use his fists. He set himself, hunched his shoulders and swung all the way from the hip upwards, twisting his torso as he did so to get the maximum amount of force out of the punch.

I slipped the guy's punch, though barely, and sent my right rocketing into his stomach. His core wasn't exactly strong enough to bruise my fist, but the punch definitely didn't have the effect I'd hoped for, and at the same time his left arm came clubbing towards my head.

I spun to my right, into and past his arm, and came back around in a full 360. The fellow was off center, allowing me to keep moving, get behind him and snap my right at him again. This time I aimed for his kidney and scored a direct punch.

The tough let out a whoof before crashing into the wall. I took just enough time for a second shot, to the same kidney, to make sure he'd stay down, then whipped back around to the door of the Richards's suite swinging wide open with the second goon nowhere to be seen.

I ran to the open door, paused long enough to whip my head in and out to get a look at the situation, then headed inside.

The living room was empty, no big surprise this early in the morning, but various crashes and groans emanated from the bedroom off to the right.

I headed straight there and right through another open door.

No doubt the second hood had assumed his buddy would take care of me. Probably a safe assumption nine times out of ten.

Entering the bedroom, I saw Dr. Richards backed up against the wall, his seventy-year old frame quivering in loose pajamas. While the hooligan was throttling the old guy, Lucy Richards stood behind him, pounding her frail fists repeatedly into his back.

Some woman.

Rushing across the room, I moved Lucy aside as gently as I could and took her place. She started to flail out at me, but must have recognized me in time to lower her arm to her side. She stepped all the way back and let me do my thing.

Only took one punch to make Thug #2 turn away from Richards to face me. But he didn't turn mindlessly. He came around, his fist already looping in my direction, but like his buddy had found out a few minutes before, I can move fast when I have to.

It took about fifteen seconds for me to get this one down for the count, and less than half a minute after that, with the help of some nylon rope that Lucy'd found from somewhere, to get him hogtied and secured in the bathtub.

All of two minutes later, I'd drug Thug #1 from outside in the hall and had him in roughly the same condition as his buddy.

"You call the cops yet?" I asked once I got my breathing under control. Forty-six years old, I reminded myself. Starting to move beyond the prime.

Doc and Lucy Richards glanced sideways at each other.

"Not yet," Lucy said.

I gave her the sharpest stare I could manage.

"Don't you think it's about time? I'm sure the front desk already has. All this had to have woken up someone. And the cops will kind of wonder why you didn't call them first."

"We don't want them involved," the doctor said, the glare he sent my way telling me that he didn't hold a lot of gratitude for my beating up two thugs for him.

"I've got news for you, doc. You remember the guard posted outside your door? Right now, he's unconscious out in the hall, and any minute now he's going to wake up from the beating these two gave him. How long before the cops come knocking?"

The two exchanged looks again.

"Mr. Quinton," the lady said, "what do you think we should do? I don't know about my husband, but I can't go on like this."

"What I think you should do," I said, "is what I've been saying all along. Tell the cops everything you know and get these goons off your back. I'm actually kind of surprised they didn't assign a guard to you guys already."

Not an idle statement at all. Especially after my latest conversation with Nichols, I would have expected to find the cops already on site when I showed up at the hotel.

Richards clasped his hands together and stared down at the floor.

"It's time you came to realize, doc, that this isn't going to end. If you keep silent, these guys are going to keep coming after you. And if you give them what they want, the other side's going to put you in their crosshairs."

Kind of a hollow threat, seeing as how the St. Louis mob was pretty much defanged these days, but the notion wasn't entirely out of the realm of possibility. And if a threat, even an idle one, got the good doctor finally playing ball, I figured it'd be worth it.

"What do they want?" Lucy spoke up sharply. "What is all this intimidation about? What do they want from him?"

She was looking straight at me. I jabbed my thumb towards her husband.

"Ask him."

"Bill," she said, turning completely away from me to focus on her husband. "What's he talking about? This goes beyond you just working for them all those years. All that time, and we never had anything like this happening in our lives. Now dead people around us, hoods breaking in and attacking. What's it all about? What is it you have that they want?"

The doc stood silently, the faintest of trembling in his frame. I wondered if he was in shock from the recent violence, mild though it had been.

At the moment, though, I didn't really care what he was feeling. And since his posture made it obvious he wasn't going to answer his wife, once again it had to be the Blond Bomber to the rescue.

And with about thirty different little puzzle pieces suddenly falling into place in my head, I had a pretty good idea what the answer was.

"It's not what, Mrs. Richards," I said, taking a shot in the dark, though in a dark that was finally beginning to lighten up. "It's who."

"Who?"

"Correct."

"Bill," she repeated, still with her back to me, "what's he talking about? What have you done?"

The good doctor slumped onto the bed and glared at me some more.

"You want to tell her" I asked, "or should I?"

"Tell me what, goddammit!"

I'd never imagined the lady as a curser, which made the words coming out of her mouth that much more harsh.

I took Lucy's hands and guided her over to an easy chair. Turning my back on her husband, I faced the lady, who clearly deserved better than she'd ended up with.

"He knows the location of Tony Lipardo," I said. "He's been treating him for the last six months."

She nodded her head, but with a vague look in her eyes. I waited her out, giving her the time she needed.

"And who is that?" she finally asked.

"He's the Mafia don of St. Louis," I said, keeping my tone as level as possible. "Several months ago, another family tried to take him over, and he barely escaped with his life."

"But how- how- what are you saying?"

I glanced over at the doctor. The old man stared at the wall, doing his best to ignore us. "It's simple, Mrs. Richards. There's a mob war going on in this state, and your husband

holds the key to winning it."

CHAPTER TWENTY-FIVE

The cops arrived a few minutes later. Nichols in the vanguard, along with Lt. Kronberg. Considering how major this thing was becoming, I figured the chief himself wouldn't be too far behind.

As the elevator opened, I stood outside the room, waiting on their arrival. Nichols rolled his eyes.

Kronberg looked like someone had kicked him straight in the balls. Always nice to be appreciated by the local officials.

"Why are you here?" Nichols asked in a firm, controlled tone. I watched Kronberg turning all different shades of color and answered my friend.

"Waiting on you guys," I said. "There's one person down, a security guard. He'll probably be okay, but he needs to get to a hospital to be checked out. Your two suspects are in the . . ."

"Suspects in what?" Kronberg, glancing back at the officers who continued to exit from the elevator, had finally found his voice. "And what the hell are you doing here, Quinton?"

I'd had a hard couple of days and didn't see how things were going to get any easier any time soon.

"I'm here to help out a client," I said. "And upon arriving I found a guy flat on the floor and two thugs about to break in. And as long as we're on it, why wasn't there a police guard for the doc and his wife?"

"Why should we have them guarded?" Kronberg asked.

"Well, way I get it, it's pretty clear that these two are right in the middle of a gang war shaping up around us. Or haven't you been keeping up with events the last few days?"

"And what have you done that's so great?" the lieutenant snapped.

I gestured at the door.

"Obviously saved their lives, more than you've done."

A grumble from the assembled cops. Most of them may have been uniforms, and all of them were lower in rank than Kronberg. Even so, questioning the competence of a higher-up wouldn't exactly endear me with the troops.

Kronberg started to make a comeback, then snarled and turned to head into the suite.

Nichols began marshaling the officers, who began moving back and forth and in and out of the suite.

The elevator dinged open, and a couple of paramedics wheeling a gurney came out.

"Where are they?" Nichols asked me.

"The bedroom," I said. "But I doubt you'll get anything out of them. She's mad as hell but doesn't know anything. I'm not all that sure, but the doc himself may be in shock."

"Shock?"

"I'm kind of guessing that he never thought it would get this bad."

"What would?" Nichols asked. "You any idea just what the hell is going on with that guy?"

I thought about my options. On the one hand, the safest thing for the Richards's would be for the doctor to reveal what he knew to the cops and take his lumps with the authorities.

Problem was that it wouldn't be just the local authorities. If my hunch was correct, and before Nichols and company arrived the doc hadn't denied anything, the feds would come down on him like the wrath of God.

I'm not a lawyer, by a long stretch, but even I could rattle off the top of my head at least half a dozen felonies Richards would leave himself open to, including harboring a fugitive and aiding and abetting who knows what.

And that was just for what I suspected he'd been up to in the last half year. If the cops really wanted to put the screws to him, they could conceivably come up with about three decades worth of charges.

And that was just one side of the equation.

The mob has this mythical aura about them that any offense, no matter how slight, will be remembered and some day, when the offender least suspects it, they'll strike back. Maybe that was true in the old days, but not so much now.

Not since RICO or Gotti.

Not since half a dozen criminal groups from various countries came in and set up shop, suddenly relegating the old boys to two-bit players on the national stage. Sure, Don Lipardo was a tough old boy who'd earned his reputation as the nastiest of the bunch west of the Mississippi, but he was an old man, his empire crumbling in half a dozen different directions. The very fact that he'd gone to Paddy for help, instead of one of the other families (of the few that were left) around the country, showed just how little stroke he had in his old age.

If the doc gave him up, and the cops came crashing through the door, sure, the old boy would be pissed, but he'd have a lot more important items on his plate than going after Richards.

This, of course, was all assuming my hunch as to his recent activities was on target.

I was pretty sure, though, that none of that would get through to Richards, and I didn't really care. I'd been hired by the doc's wife to find out just what her old man was involved in, which I'd done. I'd earned my pay, and the smartest thing to do, for both the Richards's safety and the goal of keeping my own health and welfare intact, was to turn it all over to Nichols.

Yet I couldn't help but wonder if even police custody would be a safe place for them. If he knew where the don was hiding out, then it wouldn't be Lipardo coming after them.

Rather, it would be the KC mob gunning for him.

My only real confusion was as to exactly where Paddy figured into the whole thing.

When it came down, which side would he cling to?

And then there was Lt. Kronberg. As I stood off to the side and watched things unfold within the suite, I couldn't help but wonder just why there hadn't been a police guard on the doc and his wife the whole time. With the discovery of LeBow's corpse, it should have been obvious that something was coming down, and standard procedure should have been to post a guard on two of the principals involved. Instead, Kronberg had done nothing.

As I watched him now, he strutted around seeming to oversee the processing of the scene, but to an experienced eye he was just getting in everyone's way.

I pulled Nichols by his sleeve and took him around a corner in the corridor.

"Got a proposition for you, buddy," I said.

"Not interested," Nichols interrupted. "Unless your proposition is that you're going to tell me everything that's been going on here, all the way back to when LeBow decided to camp out in the doctor's house."

"Listen, Josh," I gave him the winning smile, the one the Blond Bomber had used right before slugging some poor sap over the head with a garbage can lid. "You've got an old lady who's scared to death but doesn't know anything. You've got her husband who, last I saw, was damned near catatonic, probably from fear."

"He deserves it. If he threw in with these mugs, over all these years, then he deserves whatever he's going to get."

"Maybe," I said. "And I'm not going to waste time discussing the metaphysics of it all with you. What I'm saying is that you've got an elderly couple that may have two different mob factions gunning for their lives, and I seriously doubt they're willing to throw in with the cops."

"You suggesting what? That you look out for them while we round up the bad guys?"

"Doesn't that make sense?"

"You do realize," Nichols said, his voice dripping sarcasm, "that we can do two things at one time, don't you?"

"Josh," I said, "Pull your ego out of it and think. St. Louis fell apart months ago. Since then the local force there, the State Bureau and the feds have been trying to get a handle on the situation, and I'm guessing so far, all three have come up short. What makes you think the Providence PD can do any better, especially considering the size of the force?"

"We're good cops." The sarcasm had given way to defensiveness.

"I know you are," I said. "Not denying that. What I'm saying is that the mob war that's been rocketing through the eastern part of the state, and all the way to Chicago, is now shifting to here. Before long, you guys are probably going to have your hands full, if you don't already. You really want to spend time protecting a couple of senior citizens in the bargain?"

"We could just throw them in a cell and have them wait it out."

"And how would the press react to that? Richards, I can see. Let's face it, he's got no one but himself to blame for his mess. But his wife's an innocent party in all this. You really want to lock her up just to prove a point?"

Nichols chewed his lip on that one, his eyes shifting from me to the floor and back again.

I let him mull it for a minute before pulling out what I figured for my ace.

"Heard anything out of Paddy?" I asked.

Nichols shook his head, looking more sick by the moment.

"Not for hours. And don't think we haven't been looking. He's disappeared from all his regular places. You ready to tell me where he is?"

I kept my face blank and my mouth shut.

"That's what I thought," he said. "You're sitting here giving me all this advice, when the whole time you could help clear up a chunk of it."

"Josh, you really think he's still holed up where he was the last time I saw him? Why would he hang around waiting to be scooped up?"

Nichols's cell phone buzzed, and he plucked it out of his jacket pocket. I wandered off a few feet while he conversed with his device.

The talk was short, with Nichols contributing no more than a couple of "Okay's" before he put the phone away and turned back to me.

"Okay, Sam. It's going to go ballistic in about ten seconds."

Even as he spoke, the elevator doors opened, and four men walked out. One, I recognized from seeing on the local news from time to time. The other three almost reminded me of the clones that had been dogging Paddy around. It only took one glance to recognize them as federal agents.

"Speak of the devil," I said.

Without another word to me, Nichols walked over and began briefing the chief of police and the other three men.

A minute later Kronberg, appearing from somewhere down at the end of the hall, rushed over to join in.

I crossed my arms, leaned against the wall and waited to see how it broke.

CHAPTER TWENTY-SIX

I didn't wait for very long. After only a minute or so, the three feds and Kronberg split off from Nichols and the chief and headed into the suite. I detached myself from the wall and started to follow, but Nichols came up from behind and grabbed my arm.

"Don't do it, Sam."

"They won't let me in?" I asked.

"Probably not. They're taking the doctor and his wife in for questioning."

"She doesn't know anything beyond what I've shared with her," I said.

"Maybe, maybe not. But the doctor sure must because there's a whole lot of crap flying around him for such an innocent guy."

Obviously, my deductions about the doc weren't as brilliantly original as I'd believed. At some point, somehow, he must have floated onto the federal radar.

Considering they hadn't even had tight surveillance on him, though, someone must have seen him as low priority.

"What are you thinking, Josh?"

"Same thing you probably know for sure."

"Oh yeah?"

"Yeah," Nichols parroted. "Richards is on their payroll, isn't he?"

"Of course."

"Whose exactly?"

"I'm still working on nailing that down. Possibly more than one faction."

The suite's door opened up, the feds and Kronberg escorting the doctor and Lucy out.

The doctor looked defiant, though still confused, while Lucy mainly seemed resigned.

"I need to go in with them," I told Nichols.

"No way, man. This is way over our level now. If Richards can give those guys what they want, it's all over."

"Get me in with them, Josh. Mrs. Richards is my client."

"She's not under arrest."

"So? She's still entitled to representation."

"She's entitled, if anything, to a lawyer. But not even to that. I told you, she's not under arrest. It's her husband they want to talk to."

By this point, the small group had made their way to the elevator and were waiting for the cage to open.

"Goddammit, Josh. Those two have had a bullseye on their backs for the last several days, and now you guys are getting ready to shine a spotlight on them as well."

Just as the cage opened, Lucy turned and caught my eye. Her face, drawn and pale, called out to me.

Nichols tried grabbing me again, but I shrugged him off and started moving forward. Kronberg noticed me as well, and before I could get there he'd grabbed both elderly people by the elbow and shuttled them inside the cage. By that point I'd come within a foot of so of the action, but one of the feds put out his hand and literally shoved me out of the way.

I snarled at him and began moving forward again, but the guy, no doubt raised on old-timers' stories about the Untouchables, pulled his suit jacket back far enough for me to see his gun.

Being a mere private citizen, I took a step back, raising my hands as I did so.

The elevator door closed, Lucy Richards still sending that beseeching look my way, and Nichols came up behind me.

"See what I mean?" he said. "This is way over our level now, guy."

"Except she's still my client," I pointed out, "and she's still entitled to representation."

"Then get her and her husband a good lawyer, and leave yourself out of it."

I turned to my cop buddy, wondering just how he could be so dense.

"There's something else you haven't considered, Josh. Something real problematic about hauling those two downtown."

"And what would that be?"

"Think about it, guy. Think about all this objectively. How did those two goons know where the Richards were staying?"

"They got the info from the desk clerk, more than likely. He's already being questioned downstairs."

"Great," I said, "so they got the room number from the desk clerk. But how did they know which hotel? Or even that they were in a hotel?"

Nichols tried to stare me down, but at the moment he didn't have it in him.

"Christ," he said, staring down at the floor.

I could imagine what was going on in my friend's head, but he had to process it on his own, and as long as I'd known Nichols, I figured he'd find a way to get there.

"You may be wrong," he said.

"I may be, but at the moment can we afford to take the chance?"

He shook his head, not saying a word.

"We're not done yet," I said. "We've got to proceed with the assumption that they turned someone in the PD. Providence has a dirty cop. And I've got a possible number one candidate in mind."

CHAPTER TWENTY-SEVEN

Providence doesn't have an FBI branch office, and it turns out the three feds who showed up at the hotel were the vanguard of a strike force out of St. Louis. Due to the lack of offices, everyone scuttled themselves over to the central P.D. building, and the waiting game began.

Following the official train, I managed to get as far as the ground floor lobby in time to see everyone else heading upstairs. I thought of calling Lucy on her cell phone, if she even had it with her, but figured that wouldn't do anything but piss all those guys off. The best I could do was grab a cup of coffee, plant myself in one of the hard plastic chairs arrayed along one wall, and wait for developments.

Technically, I guess someone could have told me to get the hell out of there, but with everyone involved in the case upstairs, no doubt wishing they could take Richards back in time to the old rubber hose days, the uniforms who occupied the various desks and counters pretty much ignored me.

Some hours had gone by before Nichols stepped out of an elevator and headed my way. I slugged down the rest of my umpteenth cup of coffee and got up to meet him.

"Well?" I asked.

Nichols shook his head and headed out the front door. I followed him, and we walked until we got to the other end of the block.

By this point, we were getting on towards early evening. The temps had been in the low seventies earlier, warm for so early in the year, and with the sun on the verge of setting the mild heat had dissipated, leaving a slightest trace of coolness in the air. On nights like this, hordes of people often thronged the downtown area. Going to and from eateries, darting in and out of the small shops that lined the streets, or just wandering around. For now, though, the business activity of the day had pretty much wound up, and the entertainment phase of the evening hadn't really begun yet. So only a few people, none of whom bothered to look our way, walked past Nichols and I as we hung out on the corner.

"Exactly who's the client?" Nichols asked when we reached the corner. "The old man or his wife?"

"The wife," I said. "I wouldn't give the time of day to the doctor. What's going on in there?'

Nichols shook his head.

"About like you probably guessed it," he said. "Richards has been on retainer for going on thirty years now. First with Kenny Smith."

"I've heard of Smith," I said.

"Yeah," Nichols grimaced. "He was a hell raiser in his day. Then, when Kenny retired and turnkeyed his operation over to O'Brien, Richards automatically became part of the deal."

"An on-call medic," I said.

Nichols nodded.

"He couldn't have had all that much to do in this territory," I pointed out.

"That's pretty much how he says it. According to the old man, he only got called out once or twice a year, usually for minor injuries that occurred during, shall we say, transportation activities. Once or twice he had to treat gunshot wounds, and I guess Paddy figured those infrequent instances were worth whatever he was paying the doc each year."

"What did he make overall?" I asked. Nichols shrugged.

"Who knows? The feds don't really care about the money, they just want what he knows. What brought this all to a head."

"Lipardo," I said.

Nichols reached up and rubbed the back of his neck.

"The don's been missing from St. Louis for months. There was a shootout at his home, but he vanished from there. Everyone figured he was either dead or gone somewhere far away."

"But he didn't go very far at all, did he Josh?" I asked.

Nichols shook his head and turned to look down the street.

Opposite from where we stood sat the Bar-B-Q joint I'd eaten at the night I brought Nicky into the station. You couldn't tell from the outside, but inside the place only held four booths and a half a dozen stools at a low bar. Outside were two wrought iron tables with matching chairs. A young couple sat at one of the tables, chowing down on ribs. The girl stayed fairly neat, but her companion had sauce running down his chin.

"No, Sam," Nichols said. "He didn't go far at all."

My buddy turned to face me.

"But he was hurt, according to Richards, hurt bad. And he's been here in Providence the whole time."

CHAPTER TWENTY-EIGHT

"How much did they let you in on?" I asked Nichols. Another shrug, plus a frown.

"I got to be in the room, seeing as how it's my case that started all this. But I wasn't allowed to ask any questions or take any part in it."

"Seen but not heard," I said. "Got that right."

"What's going on now?"

"Right about now, there's more high-powered law enforcement presence up there than I've ever seen at one time. I mean even from back when I worked in St. Louis. There's fed, state, county and city in there."

"All just arrived?" I asked.

Nichols frowned.

"A few," he said, "but the greatest bunch of them just wandered in during the last few days."

"Tammy Dodger's death got the locals started on it," I began.

Another grimace, deeper than before.

"For us, sure. But it turns out that there's been rumbles for a while about Lipardo hanging out in some other part of the state. Listen to some of those guys talk, especially the Washington ones, and you get the idea KC and St. Lou are the only two cities we have."

"So now?"

"Right now, Richards is giving them chapter and verse."

I mused on that one for a while, at the same time wondering why I cared. After all, my part in this was done, at least as far as gainful employment was concerned.

"He's telling them where to find Lipardo?"

"Turns out when he lit out from St. Lou he headed this way towards Paddy. Way Richards tells it, the don's boys, the few left alive, did a slapdash job of bandaging him up and barely got him here alive."

"And they went to Paddy for help?"

"Uh huh," Nichols said. "And our local Irish ganglord just happened to have a spare medic on call and . . ."

I did some quick putting together of two and two.

"He's been treating Lipardo all this time," I said. "While most of the world thought the man was dead."

Nichols nodded.

"Which means he knows where Lipardo's holed up. Or at least where he was recently."

He nodded again.

"And they managed to sweat it out of him?" I asked.

"From what I hear, it didn't take a whole lot of sweating. The man's old, after all, and he's been through ten different levels of anxiety for the last few days, ever since we called him about the dead girl in his house."

"And they probably let his wife stay by his side," I said, "telling him over and over to just tell the truth so they could get on with their lives."

"That wife of his is really something," Nichols said. "She hired you to figure out his story, right?"

Now it was my turn to nod.

"I'd say you did your job and can walk away from it now."

As he spoke, a flash of movement down the block caught my eye, and I turned to see seven or eight black SUV's leaving the PD's parking garage and heading south, towards Broadway.

"What about the other side of it?" I asked.

"What other side?"

"That's your strike force, heading out to take down Lipardo."

"If they get lucky, yeah. But it's not my strikeforce buddy. Everyone on top made very clear that I'm just a bystander in this."

"Bully for the feds," I said, "but where does that leave us?

"I'm telling you, Sam. They didn't exactly confide in me. But that was an awful lot of manpower we just saw head out."

I stared down at the sidewalk for a moment.

"Where does that leave the Richards?" I asked.

"In custody for now. The old man for sure. As for the wife—"

I glanced up at my friend.

"Arrested?"

"Not yet, but I'd bet that the doctor's going to be charged with something eventually."

"Despite the fact that he's turned over one of the top dons in the Midwest?"

"They'll probably throw that in as mitigating, but he still danced with the devil for an awful lot of years."

"His wife?"

"Dammit, Sam, how should I know? Keep in mind, we're talking federal prosecutors here, not us local yokels. Far as I could tell, she's clean as can be. But I was out of the room more than in it."

A couple in their twenties, walked by, holding hands and walking a large German Shepherd. The dog had a prominent black mask and sharply-pointed ears, and as they walked the two of them kept bumping their shoulders together.

"What you're saying is there's going to be a whole lot of action tonight, right?" I asked.

"Probably into tomorrow morning as well," he said. "They sweated everything they could out of the old man. From what I hear, he made a point to keep his eyes and ears open all those years."

"What about Paddy?"

Another shrug.

"I'm guessing the feds consider him more our problem than theirs. If they come upon him, fine. But they're primarily interested in Lipardo and, to a lesser extent, the KC group."

"KC has been running Paddy for months now. If the feds round them up, he'll probably end up in the net as well."

Nichols rolled his eyes.

"What can I say, Sam? You think anyone in this part of the state is going to cry if Paddy O'Brien gets snatched up?"

Although we'd been standing in the same spot for several minutes now, I suddenly noticed the smoky, rich smell coming from the Bar-B-Que place across the street. My stomach growled, and I tried to remember the last time I'd eaten anything.

"For sure, it'll be an interesting twenty-four hours or so," I said.

"No doubt."

"What about what I mentioned earlier?"

Nichols sighed and something seemed to deflate out of him. His shoulders slumped, and a new kind of looseness appeared on his face.

"You don't believe that, Sam."

"I don't? Somehow those hitters found out where the doc and his wife were staying. How could they have done so without someone on the inside?"

"Hell, we're not that big of a town. There's only so many hotels in the area, and if they went about it methodically . . ."

"Or they could have just bought someone in the department and gone about it that way. Don't be naïve, Josh. Buying off cops is one of their standard tricks."

His face darkened, and even in the evening gloom I could see his nostrils flaring. I couldn't tell if he was angry with me for making the suggestion or himself for not wanting to believe it.

"The hell of it is, it could be anyone. In a force as small as ours, almost everyone not in uniform knew where they were."

"And probably most of the uniforms."

"Okay, what's your suggestion?" Nichols asked. "Just to be safe, we need to get them out of there."

"Why? The doc's already given up the info to the feds. What would be the point of messing with them now?"

I linked my fingers and stretched my arms above my head, feeling the ligaments crinkling. I needed to get to the gym sooner or later. I hadn't had a decent workout since LeBow had come traipsing into my place.

"Two things," I said as I lowered my arms back down. "How do we know he's given up all he knows? He's worked for them what, thirty years? He could have all kinds of knowledge tucked away that he's holding out on for now. Also, you know as well as I do that the bad guys aren't above simple revenge, even if they get nothing out of it."

"But which bad guys? St. Louis? Paddy's crew?"

"My best guess would be the KC bunch. Lipardo's been on the run for so long that his organization's practically collapsed. And aside from the don, who connected with St. Louis has Richards had any contact with? He was Paddy's sawbones, after all."

"You forgetting Paddy was controlled by Lipardo's crew?"

"From a distance," I said. "No reason for Richards to have any contact. He probably never heard the don's name until he showed up here to get treatment. By the way, learn anything about just what happened to Lipardo."

"Not much, at least not while I was in the room. But I gather it was a sit-down that went bad, with only Lipardo and one or two of his crew getting away."

"How bad was he hurt?"

Nichols shook his head.

"Didn't hear."

"Even so, we've still got the problem of Richards and his wife as possible targets."

"Crap," Nichols spit out, his fists bunching in front of him.

"We can't take the chance, Josh. If someone is on the inside, the doctor and Lucy are in danger. We've got to get them out of there."

He turned to face me, his expression harder than I'd ever seen.

"And just how do you propose we do that? And what makes you even think I'd go along? You're talking about springing federal prisoners from custody. You may not have a career and pension to think about, but I do."

I paused, various arguments running through my brain.

"So, let's do two things at once," I finally said. "Let's get the Richards to safety and flush out the inside person."

"Like I said, how?"

That one had me stumped because, at the moment, I didn't have the damndest idea just how to go about it.

CHAPTER TWENTY-NINE

We finally figured it out. I made a quick phone call to Bernie Lyman to get the ball rolling, then Nichols and I headed back to headquarters.

Lyman showed up at the PD building about eight, waving a court order he'd managed to somehow acquire after hours and demanding the immediate release of Bill and Lucy Richards.

"I want to see my clients, and I want to see them now!" Lyman insisted to anyone without earshot, and he made sure practically everyone on the ground floor was.

Lyman's a short guy, something under five seven. He weighed about one forty several years ago when I first met him, and he weighs about the same now. According to Duke Prowder, Lyman had weighed one forty when they attended high school together back in the Dark Ages.

He doesn't look like a lawyer; more than anything he comes across as a homeless person.

Or, if we were about sixty years in the past, a hobo. With wildly unkempt hair pointing every which way (the gray I noticed about the only visible sign of advancing age), clothes that any self-respecting vagrant would think twice about wearing, and teeth stained a faint brown from years of smoking, he looked about as far from a lawyer, let alone a good one, as you'd ever think to find.

In its way, that perception is spot on because Bernie Lyman isn't a very good lawyer. He's a fantastic one.

He's been around forever, or at least since the late seventies, and scuttlebutt has it that he's never lost a case. I'm not sure if the last is true, mainly because I'm fairly confident Lyman himself started said story. But it's possible he's never lost a case in court because, and he told me once that this was the true secret to being a successful attorney, a really good lawyer, guilty client or no, would do his damndest to see that his client never got as far as a trial.

So, no, he didn't really look the part, but that had never bothered me much. After all, if you think someone like Lyman's a sight, you should get a look at the characters who lurk around the smaller wrestling promotions. Compared to some of them, Bernie looks like a member of the aristocracy.

By the time Lyman came marching into the PD building to do his stuff, Nichols had long since gone upstairs, so as not to be associated with what was about to take place. I slouched way down in one of the hard plastic visitor's chairs in the lobby and sat back to watch the show.

"I demand the immediate release of William and Lucy Richards," Lyman hollered for the fourth or fifth time. All this time, the officer manning the desk out front had been on the phone, and as he hung up he made a shushing gesture towards Lyman.

"I will not be shushed!" Lyman shrieked, even louder. Before he could say anything else, another uniformed cop, a brunette woman wearing sergeant's stripes, came down the stairs.

She hurried over to Lyman, and the two of them conferred. Most of the time she spent talking and Lyman spent waving his paperwork. After about four minutes of that, the sergeant turned back and headed upstairs, while Lyman waved me over.

"Sergeant Robard's definitely pissed," he said when I got there. "But I don't think she's pissed at me so much."

"Who then?" I asked.

"Probably the federales. Cops in the bigger cities are used to dealing with those self- righteous assholes, but out here in the sticks it's a rarer experience."

Few people I knew, besides Lyman, would qualify Providence as "the sticks," but I let it go.

"I'm guessing Robard feels like she's having to babysit the feds' prisoners?"

"You're guessing right, but she's insisting they aren't prisoners, that they can leave whenever they want."

"Yeah, right," I said. "Just walk out the door, with half the mob guys in the state roaming looking for you. Isn't that kind of like throwing the door open for a burglar with your Rottweiler in plain sight?"

"More or less," Lyman sighed. "Anyway, I'm not sure they'll be able to walk out, but the sarge did say that we could go upstairs and talk to them."

"Both of us?"

"Of course. After all, you're the one the wife actually hired. I'm just along because . . . tell me again, Blondie, why am I doing this?"

He knew damned good and well. Hell, he'd agreed to it over the phone. But I guess that, lawyer to the end, he just wanted me to confirm it so we'd have no disagreement down the line.

"You're doing this so that I'll owe you a favor, and down the line I'll repay that favor."

"With some free investigative work," Lyman said, smiling.

"Not to exceed the amount of billable hours that you spend on this case," I pointed out.

Lyman grimaced for a moment before covering it with a grin.

"Of course, my boy," he said. "That would only be fair."

* * *

Even with the court order, with all the jurisdictions involved, all wanting their bite of the apple, it took some doing, but late that night we got Dr. and Mrs. Richards out of there. It helped that the feds, for some reason (no doubt the individual urge for glory), had charged out of the house leaving only one of their number behind to guard their key witness. I guess they naturally assumed the Providence blues, or at least the state cops hanging around, would be more than happy to spend precious time guarding my client and her husband.

Yeah, right.

Even so, it took a lot of sweat and effort for Lyman to get them sprung. Complicated, in large part, by the fact that headquarters, on Friday night, was hopping. All night long people, both uniform and plain clothes, flowed in and out, and from little snatches I heard here and there it sounded like the hunt was going a bit more difficult than the Washington folks had first imagined.

Still, by the time we got out of there the vibes in the place made it clear progress was being made.

"You're going to be the babysitter?" Lyman asked me as we stood alongside my borrowed Mustang, the Richards's slumped in the back seat.

"For a while," I said. "I'll deposit them somewhere safe. By my reckoning all of this will take a day at the most."

"And by this time tomorrow it'll be safe for them to show themselves?"

"Let's hope."

As we spoke, a dark-colored SUV pulled up and four men and two women charged out. In the dark I could barely make out the letters stenciled across the back of their windbreakers.

"Think they got word?" I asked.

Lyman shrugged. "Maybe. Or maybe they forgot their target list. Or someone needed to take a piss."

I grinned.

"And all six have to go in?"

"You gotta know these feds, Blondie. They need three people, plus a Federal court order, just to tie their shoe laces."

I glanced at the passengers in my car. Lucy looked calm, but Bill Richards still gazed blankly out the window.

"Wherever you take them," Lyman said, "make sure it's way off the beaten path."

"That's exactly what I have in mind."

CHAPTER THIRTY

"Are you taking us home? Or back to the hotel?" Lucy Richards asked as we headed towards the interstate.

"No ma'am," I said. "There's going to be twenty kinds of hell going down for the next few hours, and I want the two of you to be as far under the radar as possible."

The old gal nodded her head and settled back into the seat cushion. She and her husband sat side by side in the Mustang's rear seat, but I couldn't help but notice that they sat with a six-inch gap between them, and despite the spate of violence that had occurred around them earlier, they made a point of not touching each other.

The lady had hired me to do a job, which I had, even though I wasn't feeling all that good about it right now. The way I figured it, I had this last task to perform for them, then my hands would be washed clean of the matter, at least in regard to the doc and his wife.

There was still the whole issue of Nicky LeBow, and I still felt as if I owed something to the poor guy.

"Are we staying in the city?" Mrs. Richards asked.

The doctor hadn't spoken a whit since leaving the hotel.

"Just for a while. We're going to swing by the gym to rest up a bit and grab some supplies for you two. Then, once the night's passed, I'll take you to the real hideaway."

"How long will this take?"

Of course, I had no way of realistically answering that. When it came to the multi-pronged operation unfolding, what the hell kind of inside track did I have? Nothing more than what Nichols had told me, and he'd admitted that most of the decisions going down were over his level.

Far as that went, despite our friendship I couldn't be entirely sure that Nichols had been on the level with me.

Even so, I wanted to reassure the old gal as much as possible. As for her husband, beyond basic humanity, I really couldn't care less about him.

"Should be over by this time tomorrow," I said. "With the information your husband gave, the cops will round up Don Lipardo, along with taking out the faction going against him."

I didn't even want to let on my suspicions regarding the police force. That would have only served to put her even more on edge. Someone a little more familiar with how the system worked would wonder why the two of them wouldn't be safer in the main police building downtown, but I was banking on both of them being discombobulated enough that their basic logic wouldn't kick in, at least for a while.

"We'll be able to go home, then?"

"Should be able to, Mrs. Richards. Hang on a little longer. This is almost over."

Which just proves that the old Blond Bomber wasn't quite as smart as he thought he was.

CHAPTER THIRTY-ONE

"Ericksburg," Lucy Richards said a few hours later.

I grinned at her in the rear-view mirror, though in the early morning murk she may not have seen it.

"You know anybody who lives out here?" I asked.

She shook her head, but answered in the affirmative.

"A few old friends from way back. But nobody we've seen for several years."

I nodded, pleased with my choice.

Ericksburg is a dot on the map about twenty miles northwest of the city. Home to less than five hundred people, the hamlet is best known for several antique stores and a handful of bed and breakfasts. It's kind of a weekend getaway spot for people who live in the city but find themselves drawn to a rustic way of living. Situated on the west bank of the Missouri River, and a ways off the beaten path, I figured it for the perfect place to hide the Richards away for a day or so until all the trouble shook itself out.

I seriously doubted that any of the KC boys had heard of the place, and even if they had they'd have no reason to think my client and her husband would run there.

Paddy, as far as I knew still on the wind, had lived around the area his whole life and no doubt knew of Ericksburg, but I couldn't see any reason he'd have to connect it to either me or his missing medico.

So, yeah, I felt pretty safe dropping the two of them off there.

Turning off the county highway and entering the hamlet's outskirts, the speed limit drops to about fifteen. At night, you'd be crazy to drive any faster because no one in the place has ever heard of streetlights.

Early in the morning, with the sun easing up behind us, ours was the only vehicle on the road and, except for one or two stray cats stretching by the curb, I could see no signs of life.

The main street only goes for about three blocks, with houses on one side and a scattering of businesses on the other. Not an interior light to be seen. Just too darned early for the slower pace of life you can still find in little places like this.

There's a small patch of state park on the south end, next to the river, and more houses make up the rest of the town. I made a left turn off of Main and drove about three blocks south, pulling up outside of a dark blue, second-story house that, judging by the wooden porch swing and ornamental widow's walk, seemed to have leapt right out of the nineteenth century. A small sign in the front yard announced it as Angie's Place , a not too original name for the establishment.

We exited the Mustang, Doc Richards shuffling behind me and his missus. He still had that dopey look, and as far as I could tell he hadn't yet recovered from the shock of the attack in his hotel room.

According to Nichols, Richards had been talking to the cops up on the top floor of the police headquarters, but I couldn't help but wonder just how coherent he had come off.

Unless he was a whole lot better actor than he appeared.

That actually was another reason for deciding to stash them in Ericksburg. Without a vehicle and at least twenty miles from a town of any size, if Richards decided to make a run for it he couldn't get very far.

As we stepped onto the porch, the front door opened and an old woman came out to greet us.

She looked to be in her early sixties, though I knew for a fact she was at least seventy.

She was five feet tall, with straight posture and bright blue eyes. Despite her years, only a wrinkle or two here and there, plus a slight wrinkling of the back of her hands. Her hair color, a shiny silver, I knew to be entirely natural. Sixty years ago, she would have been called a "handsome" woman.

Those blue eyes twinkled when she saw me.

"It's about time you came around, Blondie. What do I have to do to see you more than once a year?"

Shrugging, I did my best not to blush.

"Sorry, Angie, but it's been a hell of a year and running two businesses . . ." I stammered to a halt.

Angela Logan was finally living her dream of running a small-town bed and breakfast. Her husband, Howard Logan, otherwise known as "Howie the Hammer," had been a one-time wrestler who realized he could make more money, though not much more, by starting up and running his own wrestling federation. For nearly thirty years, he'd been the owner/operator of the Midwest Wrestling League and had served as my primary mentor when I started in the business.

Howie had even performed the magnanimous gesture of letting his biggest attraction (that would be me) out of my contract so that I could sign up with the big folks. He knew it had been my dream practically from the day a family friend had shanghaied me into a dusty St. Louis gym, and as far as I could tell, he'd never once even considered holding me to my obligation.

Six months later, when I had a chance to compete for the big time's greatest championship, Howie had been the first person I'd called. We hadn't had a chance to speak since parting ways, and something in his voice had sent up a warning flag.

The next morning, I'd called Angie on the QT and gotten the scoop on what his latest physical had revealed, and three months later, Howie the Hammer passed on.

Angie tried to run the MWL on her own, but after the big guy's passing her heart just wasn't in it. A year to the day from his death, she'd sold the whole shebang, pulled up stakes from

St. Louis, her home of nearly forty years, and traveled on down the road to Ericksburg.

One real estate transaction later, she was enjoying retirement as the owner/operator of a bed and breakfast.

"So, are these the two new boarders you called about?" Angie asked.

"They are," I said. "I need you to do me a favor and put them up for a day or so. But this has to be kept very quiet. No talking to anyone at all that you've got someone staying here."

Angie gave both Lucy and the doctor a once over before turning back to me.

"These folks in some sort of trouble, Blondie?"

"Big time," I said, "but there's no reason it should blow back on you. No one knows where they are but me, and I should be able to call by sometime tonight and give the all clear. You comfortable with that?"

Angie snorted.

"Comfort's got nothing to with it, kiddo. But don't worry about it, they'll be okay."

She opened up the door, reached somewhere around the inside window frame, and came out with a .357 Magnum. I recognized the gun. It had belonged to the Hammer, and I knew that, a gun lover all the way, he'd taught his wife all about shooting. Despite the size of the weapon, I knew she could handle it if she had to.

Nice, I thought, while silently praying the old girl wouldn't have to use it.

"Listen to me, Angie," I said. "If by any chance someone should come around this way, don't try to take them on. Just lock yourself away and call the sheriff. Then call me."

Angie looked like she wanted to snort, but must have thought better of it. Her eyes hooded over a little.

"It's that bad, Blondie?"

I nodded.

"You don't have to do this, Angie. Like I said, there's no way it should trace back, but there's always a chance and actually," I paused, half a dozen thoughts running through my head. "Hell with it. I'll take them somewhere else. Never should have . . ."

"The hell you will, Sam Quinton. You say there's no way anyone knows, and I'll buy that. I don't know what all is going on here, but it's obvious that you've got something a lot more important to be doing than bodyguarding these two. You go do your thing, and I'll just . . ."

"We are not staying here!"

Both Angie and I turned to see Lucy Richards staring at her husband. Seems the old boy had finally found his voice.

"No way!" he said, even more forcefully, this time looking me square in the eye.

"Dr. Richards," I began, wondering if the old man's mind had sprung a gasket. "You're in trouble, and right at the moment I need you away from . . ."

"I didn't ask for any of this," he snapped back. "I don't know who you think you are, or what my wife told you, but I'll be damned if . . ."

I took a step forward, tensing my arms enough that he could see my muscles bunch even under my leather jacket. I didn't cock my fists, thinking that would be going overboard, but I tightened my shoulders enough that the jacket cinched tight around me.

No way was I about to hit a seventy-year old man, but I was counting on the idea that he couldn't be entirely sure of that.

In the corner of my eye, Lucy Richards looked a little pale, but I couldn't worry about her just then. I had to impress on the good doctor the degree of my seriousness.

"Listen to me," I told him. "You did ask for this. You've been playing games with these guys for years. All because you wanted to lead a cushier life. Well you got that life, and now it's coming around to bite you in the ass. These people are serious, goddammit. Forget the cops and feds. With it all coming down, the KC bunch is going to tear this whole area apart looking for Lipardo, and Paddy as well. And they'll do their goddamndest best to track down anyone who can give them even a hint."

"O'Brien . . ."

"You old fool! O'Brien's in with them. Haven't you noticed all those sleek, corporate type guys hanging around him the last months? That's the modern mobster, doc, and Paddy's either sided with them or too damned scared to go against them. What do you think the dead girl being left in your house was, doc? An early birthday present?"

He blanched and began to tremble. My insides curdled. Verbally beating up an old man wasn't my idea of a fun time, but somehow, I had to get through to him.

"The girl?" he stuttered out. "What's she got to do with this?"

Now I did feel like slapping him.

"We've already been through this, doc. Or weren't you listening earlier? She was a warning," I said. "You and the missus were supposed to discover her when you got back from your overseas jaunt. I guess they assumed the message was obvious."

He paled even more, and I held out hopes that I was finally getting through to him.

"So, at the moment," I continued, "it doesn't really matter to me what you want or don't want. What I want is you safe, and what I need is your wife safe."

"And you don't think the police can take care of us?" Mrs. Richards spoke up, her voice quavering.

"Mrs. Richards," I said as levelly as I could, "we discussed this already. Off the grid is the best possible place for you to be for the next few hours."

"Because you suspect someone in the police department?" she asked.

"They did find their way to your hotel."

With that, the conversation dribbled to an end. Angie took both the Richards by the arm and led them inside. She paused in the doorway, turned and gave me a wink.

Good enough, I thought as I climbed into my car. Now to wrap this damned mess up.

CHAPTER THIRTY-TWO

I hit the city limits about fifteen minutes later. Coming in from the west, I had the morning sun in my eyes. As I took the exit off the Interstate and onto Arena, I couldn't help but realize, for the umpteenth time, that I just couldn't get used to all the traffic, even this early in the morning.

Over the last decade or so Providence's population has grown by about a third, and as some of us old timers tool around the area we can't quite imagine where all the new people came from. Between the months of August and May, it's even worse.

As I headed down Arena, I began thinking about the activity of last night and, I assumed, this morning and wondered just how long it would take the local media, and by extension the citizenry itself, to realize that we were smack dab in the middle of possibly the largest mob roundup the country had seen in decades.

As far as I knew, aside from safeguarding the Richard's, I was now out of it. I felt a bit at loose ends, though. While I'd managed to more or less figure out the lay of the land, I hadn't nailed Nicky LeBow's actual killer. Nor the killer, if someone else, of Tammy Dodger.

I pulled into the gym's parking lot and shut off my car, then sat there for a while and drummed my fingers on the console, playing a solitary game of "what if."

Just what would have happened, I thought, if LeBow hadn't

decided to crash the Richards's house? Would the doc and missus have stayed in France for a month, their stated plans? Or would they have been forced back for some reason? Probably the latter.

The idea, as I saw it, was to have them come home to find a brutally-murdered young woman in their house. While Lucy would have been confused and, naturally, frightened, the doctor would get the message loud and clear.

Give up Lipardo, or something similar happens to you.

But Nicky had screwed the works by getting locked out of his apartment, forcing him to find a place to "squat" for a few days until his luck could turn. So instead of an elderly couple, helpless to defend themselves, it had been perpetually down on his luck Nicky LeBow who'd come "home" to find the dead girl.

The message was still received, if a bit deflected. But it had been received not just by the intended recipient, Doctor Richards himself, but, in a very indirect way, by the Providence P.D.

Thus, our current situation.

I shook my head, shrugging to get kinks out of my back and shoulders, and exited the Mustang.

My intent for the day was to lay low in the gym, getting some honest work in for a change, keep an eye and ear on the local news, and wait for Nichols to call and tell me it was a wrap. It sounded like a pretty good plan, all things considered.

Nope.

I came in through the front doors and saw Lisa, wearing a black spandex uni, coaching a woman on one of the Nautilus machines. Lisa saw me enter and waved me her way. She gave a few more instructions to the client, before patting her on the shoulder and heading towards me.

"Haven't seen you for a while," she said.

"Been busy," I replied, "but things should quiet down before too long."

"Anything that has anything to do with the gym?"

That was my Lisa. Sometimes, hearing her talk the place up, I got the feeling she should own the place instead of me.

"Not as far as I know. Why do you ask?"

She jerked her thumb towards the back hallway that led to my office. "Someone's waiting to see you. Been here since I opened up."

My shoulders tensed up, and I felt the hair on the back of my neck rise. "Anyone I know?"

"Yep," she said. "And boy, he doesn't look good at all."

With that cryptic statement, Lisa turned her back on me and went back to helping the woman at the Nautilus.

* * *

It was Paddy O'Brien sitting in my office. And Lisa was right. He didn't look well.

Both his hair and beard looked limp and greasy, yet all tangled up at the same time. He had a slump to his shoulders that I'd never seen before, and a tick jackhammered under his right eye.

The big Irishman had been sitting behind my desk, but stood up when I entered. I nodded to him and slung my jacket across one of the client chairs.

"Surprised to see me alive, Blondie?"

"Relieved," I said. "I figured you'd be sharp enough to get out ahead of it all, and looks like I was right."

I walked over to one of the filing cabinets and picked up a pot of coffee that Lisa always had percolating for me each morning. I lifted the pot towards Paddy, but he shook his head.

Shrugging, I poured a cup and added my usual two spoons of sugar. Caffeine and sugar. Just what I needed after the last several days.

"You bet," Paddy said. "Got out ahead of it all but not, I think, for very long."

He started to come out from behind my desk, but I waved him back and dropped into one of the client chairs.

"The cops get Lipardo?" I asked.

"The feds actually." Paddy shrugged. "Doesn't matter much. Even before the ambush he didn't have that long to live. Richards did his best, but the don's been on death's door for the last few months. We knew he was a goner sooner or later."

I lifted an eyebrow.

"How badly did his attackers hurt him?"

"Pretty bad, but that wasn't anything the doc couldn't patch up. If they'd only known, the KC bunch really jumped the gun."

I must have looked my question.

"Cancer," Paddy continued. "His liver. It's been eating away at him for over a year."

"I thought liver cancer took people pretty quick," I said.

"It usually does. But that old bastards's just too damned tough and stubborn to go out that easy. He's been hanging on as tight as he can."

"Think this is it?" I asked.

"You mean the government boys and girls swooping him up? Damned if I know. I'll tell you this, though. He's one of the old original goombahs. Goes back to the times of Gigante, Castellano and the rest of that bunch. No matter what they do, he'll never talk."

"His own people tried to do him in," I pointed out. "Tried to knuckle you down as well. And you two have been allies for how long? You don't think he'll want revenge?"

"'Course he'll want to get back. But he'll do it his way, the old-time way. Provided time doesn't run out on him."

"The way I hear it, the old guard of his family's either gone down or on the run. Who does he have to take care of business for him?"

Paddy leaned back in the chair and stared at the ceiling for a moment.

"You may have a point," he finally said. "His back's against the wall, and he's going to want to strike out. He may pick the only way possible. And with all the others that got swooped up last night, he'll have his pick of who to roll over on."

"Where does all this leave you?" I asked. "After all, you were playing both ends against the middle all along, right?"

Paddy leaned back a bit further and laced his hands behind his head.

"I did what I had to do, Blondie. As weak as Lipardo got, I didn't have much choice when KC came knocking."

"And he won't see that as betrayal?" I asked.

"Time will tell. I gave him a safe haven, didn't I? You have any idea how tricky it was to keep him under wraps while KC had their thumb on me? Tell you this, though. Things sure won't be like they were. Whichever side ends up losing, even if the feds take both down, I'll probably only have a year or so of free reign before someone else moves into the top slot and tries to take over."

"Maybe there won't be a top slot after all this."

"Maybe not," Paddy said. "Either way, maybe it's time for me to just fold it in and go sit on a beach somewhere."

I suddenly felt a hollow spot in my chest. Paddy was a crook, sure, and we sometimes went a year or two without running into each other. But he'd been a part of my life, on and off, ever since the beginning of my pro-wrestling days, and it would seem odd for him to not be hanging around, somewhere on the periphery.

"I'm assuming you have enough to retire on?" I asked.

The big Irishman grinned and slouched farther down in the chair.

"Not as much as you would think. Despite what some people think of me, I've actually been more in the way of a franchisee, with Lipardo pulling the strings."

I wondered if my face showed the shock I felt.

"I always thought you were top guy of your operation. I knew it was small, but . . ."

"Not small, Blondie. Try non-existent. It never was my operation. I wouldn't have lasted a week on my own, not with KC a hundred miles to the west and Chicago not all that far away either. Nope, it's been Lipardo's all the time, in spirit if not on paper. He allowed me to operate, kept the rest of the boys off my back, and in return he got the profits. I got a salary and thin, very thin, profit-sharing arrangement."

Something was niggling at my brain, trying to find its way to the surface. At the same time, I was trying to process what I'd just heard. No matter how I tried, I couldn't picture Paddy O'Brien as anyone's gopher. I'd always known, of course, that he'd had some sort of arrangement with St. Louis. As he'd said, he wouldn't have lasted any time at all as a complete independent, but I'd had no idea how much Lipardo had had hold of him.

"But before I hit that beach," Paddy was saying, "there's one more thing to take care of."

"Which is?"

"The doctor. Richards? I've got a little business with him. Know where I can find him?"

I kept my face as blank as I could.

"Last I knew he was in custody himself."

Paddy shook his head.

"No doubt he was, probably for quite some time. After all, considering the amount of information he spit out, it had to take some time."

"Paddy . . ."

"And when you consider that you were seen hanging around the PD building until early this morning, and my insider says he was released on some sort of cockamamie judge's order last last night. Well, one has to wonder."

I took a deep breath, working to calm the goose bumps spreading across me. Insider. A pretty blatant message that my hunch had been right.

In a way, it was sort of obvious. Even if he played the middle-management role he'd described, Paddy couldn't have operated all those years without someone on the inside at the PD and prosecutor's office. Quite possibly, more than one.

"But it's no big deal," O'Brien continued, "because it's not going to be all that hard to track him down. Not when you know someone who has access to specialized tracking equipment. You know, the kind someone can slip under a Mustang's bumper when no one's looking. Say, someone like a certain police lieutenant who's never been quite what he seems."

My nerves tightened even more. If he were willing to be that upfront, he must expect I wouldn't be able to make any use of the information. However, my brain didn't quite work fast enough to give me time to react.

Next thing I knew, the desk was upending in the air and tipping over on top of me. My reflexes, lulled by the casual pace of our conversation, couldn't keep up.

I managed to twist half to the side before the desk pinned me to the floor. I had one arm and one leg free, not enough to allow me to do more than wiggle ineffectually as O'Brien stood over me, a blacker expression on his face than I'd ever seen.

As Paddy loomed over me, I knew, too late, exactly who had killed Nicky LeBow.

But the knowledge didn't do me any good because his fist smashed down towards my face.

And everything went out.

CHAPTER THIRTY-THREE

I wasn't out long, just long enough for him to get out the door and out of my gym.

Lisa had heard the noise from all the way up front, hard to muffle a desk being thrown on someone.

By the time she got to the office door, I'd gotten my free arm under the desk and, with a few grunts and hisses, managed to lever the damned thing off. Standing up was a whole other matter, but finally I made it to my feet.

"What the hell?" Lisa barked as she came through the office door.

I shook my head to clear it, a mistake as about a thousand bells started ringing in my ears.

I took a few deep breaths, stood up as straight as I could and headed through the doorway myself.

Lisa, looking more alarmed than I'd ever seen her, ducked out of my way. I stopped just outside the office and looked around.

"He split," Lisa said, coming up behind me. "Saw him running out through the back exit when I came back here. What the hell, Sam?"

I ignored her, probably the first time I'd ever done so, and dug my cell phone out as I headed towards the front of the gym. Barreling through the doors, I hit my speed dial for Nichols as I ran to my car.

Voice mail came up. Cursing, I left him a terse message as I clambered into the Mustang and fired it up. I took a nanosecond to consider climbing back out and tearing off the bug, but figured the bad guys already had the worst information they could get.

I thought of calling 911 next, but by the time I explained the urgency of the situation to a dispatcher it would be all over. As I pulled out onto Arena and headed towards the Interstate, I placed one more quick call, to Angie Logan.

No answer there, either. Cursing, I shot through a special interchange construction we have called a diverging diamond, whatever the heck that means, and took the first lane to get westbound on the highway. Did the move in such a way, with the car actually rocking a bit onto the driver's side, that a medley of horns blared behind me.

Hell with them. I had to get there as fast as I could. As I sped on, the one hope ratcheting through my head was that Paddy hadn't been able to contact any of the KC crew. If most of them had been scooped up already, he may be essentially on his own. And with his old crew cut loose months ago, maybe he had no resources left. If so, Angie and the Richards's had a chance, though barely a chance.

Then again, it was obvious by now that a lot of things I thought I'd known about Paddy weren't all that true. Somewhere down the line, I'd take a moment and get quietly drunk over the memory of an old friend who, it turned out, wasn't such a friend after all. But I didn't have time for that right now

Dammit, I had to get some help out there somehow.

I hit the speed dial again, and this time Nichols's voice came on the line.

"What's up?" he asked. "I'm in the middle of booking about twenty different—"

"Josh," I cut him off, "I'm about eight miles outside of town, heading towards Ericksburg. We've got a problem."

I explained, in as few words as I could, what had just

happened. One thing to say for Nichols, he catches on to things pretty quick.

"I can start out that way, but jurisdictionally there's a bit of an issue. But we have a couple of state guys here, and while most of the feds are still out on the roundup, a couple of them are hanging around. I can send them that direction."

"What about the sheriff? Ericksburg's so damned small there isn't even a town constable."

"I'll place a call, but at the moment I'd suggest you get there as quick as you can."

Even as he spoke I'd taken the turnoff from the interstate onto the county highway heading north. The speed limit was fifty on that small two-laner, but I floored the accelerator, figuring if nothing else I could lead some deputies on a chase to get to where I needed them.

"I'm trying, Josh. But dammit, you guys have more mobility. Now get someone out there."

"Try the woman again," Nichols said, "and keep going buddy. We're right behind you."

I hung up and tried Angie again. Still no answer, not even a mailbox recording. Cursing again, I threw the phone down on the seat beside me and bent forward over the wheel, all my attention focused on the road in front of me.

CHAPTER THIRTY-FOUR

I didn't cross paths with a single cop, either county or state, on my fast trek back out to Ericksburg. On the good side, that time of the morning any traffic to be had is heading south, into Providence, so I had my side of the county roads practically to myself.

I hadn't bothered checking the time when I hung up with Nichols, but it couldn't have been more than ten minutes before I swung off the county highway and onto the small road heading into the village.

It caused me a little bit of concern. As fast as I'd been moving, I figured I should have caught up to Paddy at some point, and the fact that I hadn't made my gut constrict.

Along with the realization that the confrontation in my gym may have been a stalling tactic, to let someone else make the move on Angie's house.

A small part of my mind wondered when was the last time that the inhabitants of the sleepy little village had heard a vehicle screeching through their streets, especially in the middle of the morning. No traffic to get in my way, of course, but one or two little old ladies, out watering their gardens, glared at me.

And as I turned the corner for Angie's house, one grandmotherly type, swinging back and forth in her porch swing and looking all of ninety, managed to flip me the finger as I shot past.

So much for taking a cue from those old Andy Griffith reruns.

I jerked to a stop, bolting out of the Mustang almost before it stopped rocking. I'd grabbed my gun from the passenger seat, and in three steps was at her front door.

The door swung open at my touch, faintly squeaking on its hinges and beckoning me into the house.

I paused, gathering my breath and listening as hard as I could.

From inside the house and somewhere to the left, I heard a faint wheezing. At the same time, the distant keening of sirens appeared.

Taking a chance, and not liking that airy, bubbly sound, I ducked low and entered sideways.

Nothing in the living room, though a bit of disarray here and there. A sofa turned catty cornered to where it should be, a small end table knocked over, and a lamp shattered on the floor.

The sirens came in clearer now.

I turned to the left and went down a short hallway, two bedrooms on one side and a bathroom on the other. I was taking a chance, as I moved past a stairway, and if anyone lurked on the upper landing I'd be in trouble. But that wet, raspy sound continued, and it was time to draw this to a close.

I found Doc Richards in the second bedroom down the hall.

He was slumped against the far wall, his hand clutching a pink coverlet from a small bed that fanned out in front of him. The blood spread on his chest and trails of it down his chin showed that the bullet had hit his lung, and I was kind of surprised the old boy was still alive.

Though the bubbling wheeze coming from his throat told me he wouldn't be for long. The sirens had arrived right outside, accompanied by the squealing of tires and brakes.

Richards's face looked slate gray. His lips trembled as he tried to say something, but every time he opened his mouth another rivulet of blood dribbled down his chin.

Before I could kneel down in an attempt to hear, bodies in uniforms whirled into the room and thrust me out of the way.

I managed about two 360's before ending up in the outer hallway, the bedroom now jammed with sheriff's deputies and paramedics.

My cell phone rang.

I pulled it out of my pocket without looking, assuming it was Nichols on the other end.

"Josh?" I said.

"You find him yet?" Paddy's voice squeaked in my ear.

"Paddy," I said, trying to keep the trembles out of my voice, "what the hell?"

"The old boy sold me out. Me and Don Lipardo. Gave the cops everything he knew. So, I had to make things right before I hit the trail."

"If you say so." As I spoke, Nichols walked in through the front door. I motioned him up the stairs. "But if that's all it was, why take the women?"

"Woman, Blondie. Singular. You think I didn't recognize Angela from the old days? Wasn't about to hurt The Hammer's widow. Give me a little credit for a soft side. The only one I took was the Richards bitch."

The slur hit me like a punch. Paddy had always prided himself on being an old-time type gangster. Always true to his word, respectful to women, all that *Godfather* type stuff. Sure, it was a bunch of crap. Anyone who'd not only survived but thrived anywhere within the confines of organized crime was about as ruthless and self-centered as they come, but Paddy had always at least tried to keep up the image.

Now here he was talking like the lowest punk on the street.

"What do you want with her?" I asked, angling the phone the best I could so Nichols could listen in.

"Not much. She's just my insurance policy until I get clear of here. And don't try to trick me into saying where I'm heading Blondie. I may be old and slow, but I'm not that far gone."

"We're all slowing down a bit, Paddy."

"Maybe so, but even an old duffer like you was breathing down my neck. And then you went and sicced the cops on me. Since you got them on my tail, it's up to you to get them off. So just tell them to cool it. When I get far enough outside of the parameter the feds have around town I'll let her go. Then she can come home and care for the old man, provided he's still around."

Like a scene out of a movie, the EMT's picked exactly that moment to roll Richards out, the thin gurney sheet pulled up and over his head.

"Where's Angie?" I asked Paddy.

"If there's as much activity around there as I'm guessing," he said, "they should have found her by now. But if they haven't, I'd suggest going out into her backyard and seeing what's waiting out there."

I looked at Nichols and mouthed the word "backyard." He nodded and ran down the stairs, through the kitchen and, presumably, to the area beyond.

"What about Mrs. Richards, Paddy?" I asked. "It was her husband who messed everything up, not her. Surely it would be easier to travel without the extra baggage."

As I spoke, I mentally crossed my fingers as to my technique. A regular criminal, or psycho, if he thought someone was slowing him down, would just kill them and move on. And while clearly Paddy had gone off the rails somewhere down the line, I was hoping that his inherent common sense wouldn't desert him.

If I was wrong, I'd have Lucy Richards's blood on my hands for the rest of my life.

"Sure, it was her old man. And don't get me wrong, Blondie. I'm not after revenge, just insurance. Though I got to tell you, if my hand's forced in her regard it won't really bother me a whole lot."

Nichols and a uniformed patrolwoman came in from the kitchen area, leading a shaken, but intact, Angie Logan with them. In the early morning light, I could just make out the scarlet marks left on her mouth and wrists by duct tape. Nichols gave me a thumbs up while Angie flashed a weak smile my way before they took her out, presumably to be checked out by the EMT's.

"And besides," Paddy continued in my ear, "it's not like I have a whole lot left to lose, right?"

"But according to you, it was never yours to begin with," I said.

"Figure of speech, my boy, figure of speech. Did you get a look at the don yet?"

Nichols came back in. He made a motion towards my phone, but I shrugged him off.

"How could I have seen him," I asked. "You think the feds let me on the loop in any of this?"

Paddy chuckled, but his mirth sounded the tiniest bit frantic.

"Why not?" he said. "Aren't you going to be the big man, now? Gonna write a book? Maybe have a movie made about you?"

Nichols made another angry gesture, pointing to his badge looped around his neck by a lanyard. I waved him off and turned my back, but continued speaking loud enough for him to hear okay.

"I doubt it," I answered Paddy. "Think my photogenic years are behind me."

By now more and more cops were circling around, whispering among themselves. The rest of the house was almost entirely quiet as everything focused on my talk with the fugitive.

"So why you?" I asked. "Why didn't the don gather his boys around him and go down on his home turf?"

"Demographics, Blondie. Most of his old boys were gone, one way or another, and he didn't really trust the younger ones coming up. Got no honor, he told me once."

"Any port in a storm, right?" I said. "After all his years leading the Italians, it was a poor, simple Irishman who saved his ass."

"At least for a while."

As Paddy chuckled at that one, Nichols grabbed me by the shoulder and swung me around. His face looked meaner than I ever think I've seen it, and I held up a hand in an "in a moment" gesture. A couple of men who just had to be feds walked in the front door and made like a laser for me standing up on that upper landing.

"Richards treated him for months, then just took off? Did he lose his nerve?"

"I should have done the same," Paddy said, "but I just couldn't leave the old boy by himself, not after all those years. I owed him something."

I looked up to see the police chief coming through the door. Nichols blanched a bit when he saw his boss, and the glare the chief sent my way told me I had to wrap things up quickly.

Looking around at all the activity going on around, I wasn't surprised to find one particular person conspicuous by his absence.

"What is it you want, Paddy?" I asked in a slightly louder tone. "Safe passage somewhere? Money? What?"

"Simple," O'Brien said, and some new element had entered his voice. "I want to make a trade. Mrs. Richards for something everyone wants."

The chief had reached the second floor and took about three steps in my direction, but something in my expression must have even made him pause.

"What do you want to trade her for?" I asked. "The cops are right here. You can talk to them instead of me."

"Uh, uh, Blondie. I'm dealing with you, and if you want to see the old lady again, you'll do exactly as I say."

"I don't have all that much money, Paddy. Not enough to get you very far."

He chuckled again, but the sound held no humor.

"I don't need money, my boy. Got plenty of that stashed away where no one, especially not the feds, will ever find it."

"Then what?"

"I want to turn myself over. To you. I'll tell you the terms when we meet. You know the place. And whatever you do, for the lady's sake, no cops."

"They're kind of involved here, Paddy. It's not like I can tell them nothing to see here."

"You figure it out, Sam. Work it out however you have to, then call me back. But as soon as possible ditch your cell phone, wouldn't want them following you now, would we?"

The chief had lost his patience. He snatched the phone out of my hand and started squawking into it.

He only got about three words out before he threw it to the floor. Paddy had hung up.

CHAPTER THIRTY-FIVE

"No way," the chief said.

The three of us, the big man, Nichols and myself, were standing in Angie's front yard. Just as we'd stepped out, the chief had gotten a call from someone, muttered a couple of "uh huh's" into his phone, then hung up.

"Rest of the feds on their way," he said after stashing his phone. "We're just going to wait for them." He looked pointedly at me. "Including you, Quinton."

I shrugged.

"If you say so. But then you'll have to explain to the public how you let a sixty-year-old woman get murdered when you could have stopped it."

"Don't even try that nonsense, fella. If you hadn't of been mixing around in this, we wouldn't have to . . ."

"If I hadn't been mixing in it," I snapped back, "you'd have exactly nothing. Nothing except a dead girl murdered in a vacationing couple's home. As it is, you've got a roundup going on of most of the Mafia figures in Missouri, along with wrapping up a gang war. By tonight your name's going to be in every news report around the state. Hell, probably the country. And you want to know why you've got all this?"

The chief's face turned pink, but he managed not to lose it.

"Why?"

"Because Nicky LeBow got locked out of his apartment,

started staying overnight in the Richards's house, and was smart enough to seek me out when he found Tammy Dodger dead. If it hadn't of been for Nicky, all of this would have continued to go on right under your noses, you and the feds as well."

The chief stayed quiet for a second, kind of scrunched his face in a concentrating mode.

But the moment passed, and his scowl appeared.

"No soap, Quinton. Tell us where he is, where he's got the woman, or we'll haul you in for obstruction."

I sighed, as loudly and dramatically as I could.

"He didn't tell me, sir. If you recall, you snatched the phone out of my hand before he could. And even if he had told me, and I didn't want to tell you, that doesn't count as obstruction. As long as I don't lie or actively interfere with your investigation, simply keeping my mouth shut isn't legally considered obstruction."

Of course, I was lying right then, and I did plan to interfere, if not actively, but I didn't see the point in mentioning that.

"Maybe not. But if I want to I can sure make it a reason to have the state yank your license. Far as that goes, we'll just put a tail on you and see where you take us."

I glanced over to see Nichols shaking his head in despair.

"Tail away," I said. "I'm only going back to the gym to get some work done. You've got more manpower and resources than I do, so I'm assuming you'll call me when my client is safe?"

To that, I only got half a groan, so I got in my car and headed out of Ericksburg.

Behind me, a lone squad car pulled out, maintaining a steady hundred-foot distance behind me.

Obviously, the chief hadn't been kidding about putting a tail on me.

Didn't matter, though. The first person to hire me in this whole damned mess had been murdered because I hadn't taken him seriously enough.

And I was damned if it was going to happen a second time.

CHAPTER THIRTY-SIX

I strolled into Dorsey's shortly before noon.

It had taken me all of twenty minutes to ditch the tail the cops had put on me, both the obvious patrol car and the not so obvious pair of detectives behind them.

Either my training from Duke had been exemplary, or the budget cuts the Providence P.D. had been undergoing had really done a number on their effectiveness. A couple of cuts across town, one or two sudden U-turns and entering and exiting a car dealer's parking lot at just the right moment did the trick.

I then made my way to the gym, just as I'd told the chief I would. I assumed they'd have the place staked out but didn't let it worry me. My gym resides in a strip mall, for chrissakes, and there's so many ways in and out that it'd be easy to slip out undetected when the time came.

I spent a few hours doing odds and ends, seemingly going about a normal work day, just in case anyone was observing. About eleven thirty, I made my way into the office, spent a few minutes in there tidying up some loose ends, then snuck out.

Left my cell behind. Didn't want the feds pinging my location.

I saw it as a slim chance that some combination of all the law enforcement swirling around town, would be staking out the club, but slim was as much as I would give it.

No one in the building, as far as I could tell. In particular, none of the clones that had plagued my steps for the last several days. And the parking lot had been empty upon my arrival. In and of itself, that didn't count as proof of anything, but if Paddy had been on the level with me, which by this point was a ginormous "if," he was willing to meet me on his own.

Turn himself over, he'd said.

Give himself up to me to act as intermediary between him and the police with Lucy Richards as the bargaining chip that ensured his safety long enough for him to make his case.

I wondered just what Lucy was thinking of all this. It had only been a few days since she'd come to me, concerned about the sudden upheaval in her life, and now that life was more chaotic than ever.

The doors to the club swung open at my touch, even though mine was the only car in the gravel parking. Coming on to noon, and wherever all the dancers and customers were, they sure weren't here.

Ordinarily, the place would be at least somewhat occupied by this time.

Not today.

Despite the deserted lot, I was pretty sure that someone was in there. Even though total silence ruled the place, I felt something pressing down on me, some sort of instinctive understanding, all the way to my bones, that I wasn't alone.

Someone in there with me.

In fact, I was banking on finding two someones. And if I was really lucky, three.

Before leaving the gym, I'd put on a leather blazer, instead of my usual bomber jacket, and I unbuttoned it as I began walking through the lobby, past the ticket kiosk, and tried the main doors to the closed off club portion. They opened easily enough, and I walked in to find the stage and seating portion, as I'd figured, deserted as well.

Yeah, someone here for sure.

All the overhead lights were on, shining a full brightness

down onto the place like it probably hadn't seen since opening night, and quite possibly not even then.

Without shadows, without mutings of any sort, the area looked as dingy and squalid as one would expect. Threadbare crimson carpeting, with small divots protruding here and there which had no doubt caused more than one slightly-inebriated customer to stagger and fall; seats held together by curling duct tape; walls decorated by yellowed water stains; and moldy ceiling tiles.

The spot for romance, for sure.

The place hadn't been cleaned since the last open night, and I had to step over assorted empty beer bottles, paper cups, peanut shells and the occasional wad of chewing tobacco.

Making my way through the staggered arrangement of chairs, tables and booths, I swiveled my head back and forth, searching for some sign of Paddy and Lucy Richards.

I'd made it about halfway to the center stage area when Paddy's voice rang out.

"That's far enough, Blondie."

Freezing, I looked around to spot him. He stepped out from behind a curtain that fronted stage left, a big automatic in his hand and Lucy Richards cradled in his left arm.

The lady looked wasted, her complexion almost more pale than her husband's had been right before he died. Her eyes fastened on mine for a moment, a silent plea ringing out across the distance between us, then skittered back and forth across the room.

I sent a silent prayer for the lady to stay cool, then turned my attention to Paddy.

"So what kind of deal do you want?" I asked.

"Her for me, so to speak." He jiggled his arm, and I thought Lucy was going to collapse at the knees. "I've got a lot of info, Bomber. Maybe even more than the cops and feds can imagine. I spent thirty years nibbling around the fringes of Lipardo's mob, with KC and Chicago nibbling around mine. I can give them more names, facts and figures than they could sift through in a decade."

"They may have it already," I said. "So far, they've rounded up all of Lipardo's men, plus the KC clones, and everyone knows that omerta's only a distant myth to the younger guys."

"Not all of us," a voice sounded out to my right.

I turned to see the third person I'd expected, Lt. Kronberg himself, standing about thirty feet away from me, gun leveled at my midsection.

"Uh, Paddy," I said, "thought we were going to meet alone."

"Sorry, Sam. I can't take a chance anymore, not even with an old friend like you."

"So, let me see if I get this," I said. "You let Mrs. Richards go just as soon as you get a guarantee of safety?"

"Right. As soon as they make a deal, my knowledge in exchange for my life, and eventual safe passage, she goes free. Plus, they don't go after my money."

I frowned, glancing to the side at Kronberg. I could see Paddy wanting to make some sort of deal to save his skin, but I wondered what he had in mind for the cop.

"What the hell, Paddy? Why didn't you just tell me what you wanted in my office this morning and let me make a call. Why go out of your way to make things ten times as difficult?"

"Richards," Paddy said, and I noticed Kronberg shifting slightly to his left.

"Richards?" I asked.

"He had to pay for his betrayal. We trusted him, Lipardo and I, and he gave us up."

"He saved the don's life, didn't he?"

"Sure." For the first time I could ever remember, Paddy began thickening his consonants, speaking with a brogue. "But then he turned around and betrayed us. So, he had to pay."

"Simple as that," I said.

"Simple as that."

Kronberg slid another six inches or so to his left.

"Kill the doc, get your pound of flesh, then snatch the wife to get you off the hook," I said.

"'Bout sums it up, Bomber."

I did my best to catch Lucy Richards's eye. When she seemed to be looking at me, though in her shocked state it was hard to tell, I flicked my eyes down, then back up, as quickly as I could.

I wasn't sure, but I thought I saw a slight nod on her part.

"What makes you think I can guarantee anything, Paddy? I'm just a private citizen."

"You've got some juice, though. Know a few folks around the state. Couple of money people who are old-time fans. Far as that goes, I'll bet the lady here knows a power broker or two."

I started worrying about Paddy's mental state, even as I saw Kronberg take another step to the side. Hard to tell from the distance, and out of the corner of my eye, but I thought I saw his arms tensing a bit, and he for damned sure had crouched down a bit.

"She's just a podiatrist's wife, Paddy. And I'm just a broken-down ex wrestler. You honestly think we can do anything to help you?"

I gave the lady a quick blink of the eyes, and hoped she got the message.

"You can call your cop buddies," Paddy said. "They can work something out for me. Also, don't you still know some people in the media? In entertainment? Surely some of them can work me out a good deal."

"I doubt it, old friend. Besides, I already called my cop buddy."

A slight movement on the far left side of the room took Paddy's eyes off of me for a blink of an eye, and in that blink, I made my move.

Unfortunately, so did Kronberg.

Paddy surely realized he'd gambled wrong as his henchman swiveled in the big Irishman's direction, leveling his weapon as he did so.

I would have let it go at that, at the moment not caring much about O'Brien's fate, except that Lucy stood right in the line of fire.

I swept my hand underneath my blazer (there was a reason I'd stopped to change jackets before going to the club) and pulled one of my weapons from its holster snug against my backside.

I had to focus on the cop to save Lucy's life and could only hope that my backup was doing his job. I'd worried that he wouldn't manage to make his way inside the club without detection, but it seemed that Paddy had only brought the one henchman with him.

Kronberg was now sighting down on his supposed ally.

I managed to get a shot off just in time, causing the lieutenant to cringe downward, his own shot going somewhere into the floor. At the same time, Lucy had kept her cool and, bless the old gal, somehow managed to squirm out of Paddy's grasp and to the floor.

I turned towards Paddy, but even as I did so another shot rang out, from the back part of the club.

Paddy jerked forward, then collapsed backwards, his frame seeming to fold in on itself.

From a partition next to the bar, set along the left hand side of the room, Nichols stepped out, holding the biggest damned gun I'd ever seen.

Nodding to him, I rushed over to Lucy. She was staggering to her feet and, after one glance at what was left of Paddy, turned and buried herself in my grasp.

Nichols walked up to us, smoke still curling from the barrel of whatever the hell he was holding.

"What the hell is that?" I asked, pointing towards the automatic, which looked almost as long as its holder's arm.

Nichols grinned, though his face looked a little splotchy and pale. "Smith and Wesson 500. Birthday present from dad."

"He expect you to go hunting for elephants in Missouri?"

"Mr. Quinton," Lucy Richards, still clinging to me, spoke up.

"Yes, ma'am."

"Can we get out of here now?"

Nichols and I exchanged gazes.

"Yes, ma'am," Nichols answered for me, his face a little pale. "We'd better do just that. Blondie and I've got a lot of questions coming our way."

CHAPTER THIRTY-SEVEN

I was back to working on my bench presses. When I woke up this morning, I'd vowed that, come what may, I was going to crank out those four sets. This was going to be the day I finally did it.

But it was not to be. I was just getting started on set three when Lucy Richards walked in through the front doors.

She paused for a moment, took off her sunglasses and looked around before spotting me over in the corner. I use old fashioned free weights, something most of our clients look down on, and a while back Lisa had prevailed on me to move all of the free weight equipment off to the side, where it wouldn't juxtapose with the shiny, cam-operated and New Age looking machines that so many of Providence's supposed hard bodies preferred.

I struggled the bar back up on the rack as the lady made her way to me.

"Good morning," I said.

"Good morning, Sam. How have you been?'

I took a moment to wipe my head and neck with a sweat towel. She looked okay. Her face a little tensed up around the eyes and some smudges still showed here and there, but she had a spring in her step, which I took as a good sign.

"I saw you at the funeral," she said, "thanks for coming. You know you didn't have to."

I shrugged.

"No problem. And by the way, not to sound crass, but thanks for the check. It's a rarity these days for a client to pay on time."

She grinned, though the mirth didn't quite make it all the way to her eyes.

"Well, thanks to Bill's somewhat—unorthodox—activities I've got plenty of money. At least for now. The federal attorneys have been making some noises about retrieving my ill-gotten gains."

I snorted.

"Don't let them shove you around. Without some sort of evidence, some money trail or some such, they've no way of proving where your husband's extra cash came from. They can make all the noises about his mob ties they want, but unless they have something concrete, they've got nothing to go on. And if you need it, I know a good lawyer who could help you out."

She smiled, a bit fuller that time, then looked around for some place to sit. I got up and grabbed a folding chair from under the bench and set it up for her.

"What are your plans going forward?" I asked.

Sighing, she clasped her hands together.

"I'm not really sure yet. I'm planning on leaving town for a while, try to get my head together. I was thinking of visiting our—my—daughter and her family back east for a while."

I nodded, almost as if she had asked my approval.

"And what about you?" she asked. "Have you recovered from—what you went through?"

"Ma'am?"

"Well, it couldn't have been easy. Losing a good friend like that. I understand Mr. Nichols had some trouble with his superiors for a while."

"Some trouble" was a mild way of putting it. It's not every police officer who experiences gunning down his superior officer. The fact that Kronberg had been so definitely on the take had helped, of course. It turned out that the state bureau of investigation had been quietly digging into the lieutenant for some time, his name having come up on some wiretaps out of the Springfield area. But even with a clearly guilty man, one ready to gun down a couple of civilians, there would be constant rumors of how Josh could have handled it better.

Nichols and I had spoken a couple of times since, and neither time had Kronberg's name, or the resulting mess, come up. Nichols had gotten a lot of favorable press coverage, which no doubt helped, but I figured he'd talk about what had gone down when he was good and ready, and I wasn't about to push him.

"I'd known Paddy for a long time," I told Lucy, "but he wasn't what you'd call a friend. Up till all that happened, I considered him an acquaintance, as you would someone you only saw occasionally."

"And Sgt. Nichols?"

I wiped some more sweat from my head. My heartrate had gone all the way back down to normal, so I figured those four sets would have to wait for another day.

"Josh had a lot of questions to answer, sure, but it's hard for the brass to come down on someone who just singlehandedly saved a sixty-year old woman from a notorious gangster."

"Singlehandedly?"

Now it was my turn to grin.

"I figured it wouldn't hurt to give him all the public credit."

"Forgive me," Lucy said. "For obvious reasons I didn't follow the aftermath of all this on the news. But there is something I finally realized I need to know."

"Which is?"

She paused, her gaze bouncing around the gym. There wasn't much there to see. Middle of the morning we were about half full, with nearly three-fourths of those women. Retirees mainly, and a group of six guys who worked the graveyard shift at UPS. They tended to come in two or three times a week and put themselves through workouts more furious than most pro ball players I know.

Though the continual creaking of their knees always made me wince.

"Mrs. Richards? What is it?"

She came back to me, the slightest trace of fear in her eyes.

"Am I out of it?" she asked. "Do I have anything to be afraid of?"

I understood, and now I knew where those worry smudges under her eyes came from.

"No ma'am. Most of the various mob guys were rounded up by the feds, and while some are out on bail, they've got more to worry about than coming after the widow of a man most of them barely knew, if they knew him at all."

A small light appeared in her eyes, and I thought I saw some of the tension float away from her frame.

"You have no idea how worried I've been. This has all been so—different—for me. I just wasn't sure . . ."

I stood up and tossed my towel into a basket off by the wall. "Don't worry any more. You're all right."

"And what about you, Mr. Quinton? This was quite an ordeal for you as well."

I shrugged and looked away. It hadn't been all that bad, though I had no desire to go through anything like it again.

"I've been thinking," I said, "that two businesses to run is about one too many."

Lucy reached out and laid a hand on my arm.

"Maybe," she said, "then again maybe not. After all, if you only ran your gym, where would I be right now?"

She had a point.

I felt a slight tightening across my chest.

"Didn't do a whole lot for your husband," I said.

"Bill put himself in a position that no one could have gotten him out of. You and I both know he was doomed long before that poor woman's body showed up in our home. Nobody could have done more than you did, Sam. Don't hold yourself to a standard no one can reach."

I nodded, but that tightening of the chest remained.

"I'm not sure when I'll get back," Lucy said. "But I hope when I do I'll find you doing both your jobs and doing them the best you can."

I didn't say or do anything, just sat there waiting for the chest to loosen.

"Take care, Mrs. Richards."

"You do the same, Sam."

She squeezed my arm again, then turned away. I wanted to say something more, but just then Lisa called out, gesturing me to help her with something over by the yoga room.

I took one last look at the kindly woman who'd had so much hell descend on her life, and wondered one last time if there were something more I could have done.

She headed out, the early morning sunlight flooding in as she walked through the doors.

Some damned woman, I thought.